Throwback

OUT OF TIME

Peter Lerangis

Throwback

OUT OF TIME

HARPER
An Imprint of HarperCollinsPublishers

Library of Congress Cataloging-in-Publication Data
Names: Lerangis, Peter, author.
Title: Out of time / Peter Lerangis
Description: First edition. | New York : HarperCollins, [2021] |
    Series: Throwback ; 3 | Audience: Ages 8–12. | Audience: Grades
    4–6. | Summary: Thirteen-year-old Corey Fletcher, a time
    traveler who has transpeciated into a wolf, makes another attempt
    to fix his family tree without rupturing history, aided by Leila
    and Bee, another time traveler.
Identifiers: LCCN 2020033123 | ISBN 978-0-06-240644-6
    (hardcover) Subjects: CYAC: Time travel—Fiction. |
    Wolves—Fiction. | Families—Fiction. | Germany—History—
    1933–1945—Fiction. | Science fiction.
Classification: LCC PZ7.L558 Out 2021 | DDC [Fic]—dc23
LC record available at https://lccn.loc.gov/2020033123

Typography by Andrea Vandergrift
21 22 23 24 25 PC/LSCH 10 9 8 7 6 5 4 3 2 1
❖
First Edition

These three books were conceived shortly after the passing of my dad. He taught me that life was an adventure, and he believed in mine every step of the way. His spirit, and some of his personal experiences, animate this book series. I know that would have delighted him. He was a beloved papou to my own children, and as I become a papou myself I want nothing more than to travel in time, if only to hear his voice again. I hope I made him proud.

To Dad.

—P.L.

Throwback

OUT OF TIME

PART I
Corey

PROLOGUE

Corey Fletcher knew he wasn't supposed to eat pigeons.

But it was hard to keep himself back. The bird was so close, just a few feet away, gazing at the view from the bridge. It must have sensed Corey's thoughts, though, because it let out a baffled *coooo* and flew over the East River.

Pigeons were no dummies.

He growled and slinked onward, keeping his nose to the pavement. The wintry breeze ruffled the hairs on his back in rhythm with the passing cars. Someone had dropped a tin of chicken and rice on the pavement. Even though it was covered with flies, it smelled yummy. But he resisted.

At 3:30 a.m., traffic was sparse on the Queensboro Bridge. Behind Corey, the lights of Manhattan blazed so brightly you could almost hear them. Keeping to the shadows wasn't hard when you were on all fours. The people who were huddled under grimy blankets on the walkway remained asleep. Rats stayed clear. Cars sped by too fast to notice him.

Corey was worried most about being followed by his best friend, Leila Sharp. He could easily outrun her, but she was the smartest person he knew. She would try to find him.

He was under the sign to Northern Boulevard when he turned to look behind him.

A red Subaru bounced off the curb twice, its tires screeching. It passed him and came to a stop about twenty yards ahead. A guy in a New York Rangers jersey staggered out of the front passenger seat. The hairs over Corey's spine stood up. He crouched along the cement bridge wall and felt his own lips draw back over his teeth.

"Ho. Lee. Crap." The guy dropped a plastic cup to the sidewalk. "Jerry . . . *Jerry check this out!*"

The left rear passenger door swung open, directly into the traffic. As a yellow cab swerved out of the way, its driver leaned on the horn. He barely missed hitting a large guy who stumbled out of the Subaru.

Corey cringed. These doofuses were going to cause an accident. He stepped forward to warn them, but they screamed and leaped back into the car. As it tore away toward Queens, their legs dangled out each side.

Time to move fast and move smart. Someone was going to call 911. Or maybe 311, which was the number for reporting wacko, unexplainable things.

Like, for example, a wolf on the streets of New York City.

In other words, Corey.

Reaching the other side of the bridge, he stepped onto Northern Boulevard. The sidewalk shook as a train rumbled overhead on the elevated track. A truck pulled up to a warehouse lined with hot dog carts ready to be taken all over the city. None of the people seemed to notice Corey. If they did, they looked away. On the pre-dawn New York streets, a wolf in the shadows looked a lot like a dog.

"*There! By the drugstore!*" a voice cried out.

Corey froze. On the other side of the six-lane boulevard, a New York City police car raced toward the intersection. Ignoring a red light, it squealed into a U-turn and pointed itself toward Corey.

A siren wailed from the other direction. Backup.

The cops were moving fast. The car jumped a curb and stopped, maybe half a block behind Corey. An officer barged out the passenger door, her gun drawn. Another pulled a big wire cage and a kind of lasso from the car's trunk. They moved toward him cautiously.

The crrrrack of a gunshot echoed. The bullet barely missed Corey's ear. Maybe two inches. It hit the corrugated metal door of a shut bodega, then bounced onto the sidewalk.

Soft bullets. Probably tranquilizers.

The hot-dog-cart workers were running into the warehouse. Corey sprinted toward them. He hoped the cops wouldn't fire if humans were nearby.

Protected, Corey slipped quickly around the nearest corner. The sidewalk flew beneath him. The cars parked at the curb passed in a blur. Across the next street was a public park.

Trees. Cover. No one would be in there now.

He crossed the street and leaped through the gate. The sirens grew louder and then faded. Good. They hadn't seen him.

Racing quietly through the trees, he headed east. He didn't know how he knew where east was. He just did.

Queens was the western end of Long Island. Only

twenty-five or so miles to his destination. Twenty-five miles of private houses, of people with eyes and cell phones. They would all want to protect their families against dangerous things, like wolves. Twenty-five miles to Freeport. It called itself the boating and fishing capital of the East, according to Leila. Somewhere in that village, at an address Corey had memorized, lived Gus Fletcher. Who was once Corey's grandfather, his *papou*. His confidant and best friend. His fellow time traveler.

Papou would remember him. The old Corey. Eighth-grader Corey, the tallest kid in his class. Nearly six feet tall at the age of thirteen. The kid with the crazy imagination that everyone made fun of.

Time travel came with huge risks. Catastrophic risks. That's what Papou had told him. When you were a Throwback, the risks were off the charts.

Now Corey understood those words. His last trip into time had caused . . . well, this.

The old man had been a time traveler all his life. He had trained Corey. He would know how to deal with this. He was Corey's only hope.

If Corey could stay alive long enough to get there.

1

"Did you catch him?" snorted the deep, scratchy voice of Cosmo deSmiglia, aka Smig. "He was dreadfully fast."

"Of course I didn't catch him!" Leila couldn't see Smig, but she could smell him. He was hiding behind some wilted bushes at the edge of the Central Park's North Woods. "Why didn't *you* chase him with me? You just sat there!"

She'd been carrying Corey, but she'd set him down. To look at her phone. And then he was gone. There one minute, gone the next, a dark streak running across the baseball fields. She had tried to chase him, but by the time she gone a few steps he was a hundred yards away, headed toward the East 97th Street exit.

"So sorry." Now Smig's hairy snout was sticking out from the bushes. His tusks pointed upward like daggers, and even in the dark Leila could see flies on his face. "As a human, I was quite the runner. People wrote poems about my legs. Now, not so much."

He emerged into the streetlight, his hairy body thick and bowed. Next to him was a white, catlike creature with a snout like a beagle. "Sowwy," it said in a whispery high-pitched voice, "but you did take us by supwise."

Leila sighed with exasperation. She began pacing back and forth, words spilling from her mouth. "No, it's my fault. I shouldn't have set him down. I—I just didn't think he'd run away. I feel paralyzed. I don't know what to do. I wanted him to talk to you both. He's . . . he's one of you now. Just another time traveler who . . . who . . ."

"Twansspeciated," the cat creature said.

"Trrrransspeciated, dear," Smig corrected her, leaning heavily on the r sound. "You are not Elmer Fudd."

The creature who had once been Leila's human aunt hissed. "And you, dahling, go blow it out y— "

"I am just trying to help," Smig said.

7

"It's not about you, it's about Corey!" Leila snapped. "If they catch him, they'll . . . they'll . . ."

"Kill him, oh yes," Smig suggested.

"Stop that!" Auntie Flora said. "Um, pway tell, who is this fellow, Leila?"

"Corey," Leila replied. "You know . . . *Corey Fletcher!*"

"Yes. And. Who. Is. He?" Smig repeated, as if saying it slower made any more sense.

"Don't you remem— ?" Leila swallowed the rest of the question.

They both stared back at her, like gold and silver medalists in an ugly-pet contest.

Of course they didn't know about Corey. He had changed everything. Including their memories.

"Okay. Okay." Leila took a deep breath and explained as fast as she could: "Corey was—is—my best friend. He transspeciated, like you did. But you two—you transspeciated for the usual reasons, right? You kept hopping into the past during your own life span. You did it too often. Nature doesn't like it when you exist twice at the same time. It's weird and unnatural. So your genes freaked. And you became—"

"Fweaks," Auntie Flora grumbled.

"I didn't mean it that way!" Leila said. "What I'm

saying is, you guys did know Corey. And he transspeciated, too. He turned into a wolf."

"Well, that's dull," Smig said. "Flora and I are rather
a pair of unique beings, aren't we? A bit of this, a bit
of that—"

"He's pwobably a bit of this and that, too," Auntie
Flora said, "he's just lucky that the pieces wesemble a
wolf."

Smig chuffed away a tear. "It's a cruel, cruel pun-
ishment for those of us who become addicted to
time travel. Our only recourse is to hope for a cure
someday—"

"No! Corey didn't OD on time hops," Leila said.
"He's only thirteen, and he learned he was a Throwback just a few months ago. The thing is, his last trip
was to World War II, and when he got there—"

"Excuse me," Auntie Flora piped up. "Did you say
this boy is a Thwowback? As in, someone who can
actually change histowy?"

"And I'm the tooth fairy." Smig snorted. "Dear
child, you're old enough to know Throwbacks are
like leprechauns and fairies—delightful to imagine
but impossible. The past cannot change. It's a law of
nature. Travelers, such as yourself, your aunt, me, we

delude ourselves into thinking we can do it. Thus we keep trying, like an addiction. That, my girl, is why we transspeciated."

"Stop hogsplaining and let her speak," Auntie Flora snapped.

"Corey has the ability to change history," Leila insisted. "He stopped his grandmother from dying on nine-eleven. Thwarted an attack on his sister. But then he . . . we . . . got ambitious. We tried to keep Hitler from coming to power. It didn't work. So the mission changed, when we found this."

Leila reached into the pockets of her flannel-lined jeans jacket. Her friends liked to tease her for the dorkiness of it. But Leila was a "stuff" person, and this jacket had pockets inside and out. She was glad she'd thrown it on in her bedroom, while Corey sat on her bed under a blanket. Scooping him up and taking him here, before her mom could see him, seemed a smart idea at the time.

Her fingers closed on a credit card, phone, a small journal, and two pens. Finally she located a battered metal cigarette case. She held it out for the other two to see. "This came back from the past with Corey just now. I found it on the floor when he appeared. It belonged to his great-uncle Stanislaw. Corey learned that Stanislaw was killed in World War II. His sister, Helga, was smuggled away to South America. There, she met her future husband—Luis was his name, I think? Those two eventually became Corey's grandparents, on his mom's side. Helga always missed her big brother. They were the only two remaining members of their family."

"Ah, so Corey attempted to save Stanislaw's life?" Smig said. "This is of course what I would do."

"Yes," Leila said. "And he succeeded. But things got weird. While Stanislaw was recovering in the hospital, he was reunited with Helga."

"That's not weird, it's vewy dwamatic," Auntie Flora said. "If I could cwy, I would."

"But because they were reunited, Helga was not sent away to South America," Leila continued. "Do you see? Helga never meets Luis. They never form a family—"

"And Corey is never born," Smig said softly.

Leila let the words float into the night air, as if they would disappear and make the whole thing go away. "That's why you don't remember him," she said, shoving the cigarette case back into her pocket. "He throwbacked his own self out of existence. And your memory adjusted. It wiped him from your brain."

"Oh dear," Smig murmured.

"Um . . ." Auntie Flora scratched her snout with her left paw. "If he never existed, why do you wemember him? You shouldn't."

Leila didn't know the answer to that. It was true, she remembered everything about Corey. Their childhood playdates in Central Park, their classes together, their mornings at the Mila Café, their trips to 1939 Germany and 1908 Vienna. "But I do. The memories are all there. I don't know why."

"And yet," Smig said, "I believe this is not the only existential conundrum here."

Leila and Auntie Flora stared at him. "In plain English, please," Auntie Flora said.

"In plain English, why is he here at all?" Smig replied. "If he wasn't born, he shouldn't be here, period. No matter what form he takes—wolf, human, stalk of celery, plastic chair, I don't care. If he ain't, he ain't. Simple enough?"

Leila had no reply to that either. Her mind was turning itself inside out.

One. She shouldn't be able to remember someone who never was born.

Two. There couldn't be a Wolf-Corey if there was never a Corey.

The more she thought about it, the worse it got.

"There's a third thing," she said. "If there was no Corey, then no one could have saved his great-uncle. Which meant Stanislaw died. Which meant Helga went to South America. . . ."

"And, ipso facto," Smig continued, "Corey was born."

"My head is spinning," Auntie Flora said. "He couldn't be born, but he had to be born. Which is it?"

Leila shook her head. It was spinning, too.

There was something else she remembered, something Corey had taped to his bedroom wall in sixth grade. It was a copy of an etching by a famous artist. A staircase that connected with itself, seeming to go both up and down at the same time, in a never-ending circle. Everything in the etching made sense, but it was physically impossible. "M. C. Escher," she murmured.

"Pardon me?" Smig asked.

"The artist," Auntie Flora said, "who made the impossible possible."

Leila looked over her shoulder toward the East Side. Just outside the gate, she could get a taxi. "I'm going to find him. Somehow. If you were Corey, where would you go?"

"To the zoo?" Smig suggested. "When I first transspeciated, I thought I'd find companionship there. But the sea lions were so awfully dull. Just wanted to talk about fish, fish, fish."

"You bwought Cowey here," Auntie Flora said. "Did he say anything to you? Did he give you any hints?"

Leila thought back. "He was so broken up. He got totally squirmy and agitated, talking a mile a minute. He was hard to understand."

Smig gave Auntie Flora a look. "Uh-oh. Sounds like a possible autoimmune condition. Transspeciitis."

"Stop it!" Auntie Flora said.

"What?" Leila snapped.

"As you can imagine, with such gene irregularities, transspeciates face many health risks," Smig went on. "In my case it is minor, a chronic tendency toward flatulence. But in approximately one out of seven transspeciates, the transformation continues. They become less and less human and more like the species they have adopted. For some reason, their autoimmune functions are affected and they may weaken and die in an awful, painful way."

"*What?*" Leila began backing away.

Flora whacked Smig with her paw. "Will you stop scawing her, you blowhawd? Smig is just being alawmist and going off topic. What other things did Cowey say?"

"He—he—" Leila swallowed hard, trying not to panic. "He seemed really upset about his other grandmother, on his dad's side—the one who died in nine-eleven, the one he saved. He kept wondering stuff aloud: Was she back to being dead now? If she was alive, where was she? What happened to Papou?"

"Yesss, good question," Auntie Flora said. "If Cowey's mom was never born, then Cowey's dad must be involved in another family. Which means Papou must be somewhere else."

"Well then, perhaps Corey went to Poopoo's apartment!" Smig asked. "Er, assuming he would know where that is?"

"Papou, not poopoo," Leila said, taking out her phone, "and . . . it was awkward, but he made me look up Papou's address while we were on our way."

She held the screen out to Smig and Auntie Flora.

Q FLETCHER, GUS

Age: 73
Address:
176 McNulty Drive
Freeport, NY 11520
516-555-7519

"Freeport is across the East River and thirty miles away!" Smig said.

"Right," Leila said. "Corey wouldn't dream of actually going there, right? He'd have to take a bus."

Auntie Flora let out a sound between a purr and a hiss. "He's not Cowey anymore, deawy."

Leila shoved the phone back in her pocket.

Of course. She had to stop thinking of him as a thirteen-year-old boy. He was a wolf. Wolves didn't take buses.

They ran.

Smig and Auntie Flora had had the good sense not to follow her onto Fifth Avenue. It was creepy to be all alone on the empty street in the dark, but no one was there. And after fifteen minutes, no taxi either.

Under her breath she cursed the fact that she had no car-hailing app. It was a New York thing. In Manhattan, you just stuck out your arm. A taxi picked you up and got you to your destination while everyone else was still checking the map for their ride.

But an arm didn't work so well at this hour, when no cab was cruising the Upper East Side. She would need to download something, quick.

Honk-honk!

As she was staring at her phone, a car pulled to the curb. "Which app are you using?" called a voice. "I use all of them!"

A young woman smiled at her through the open window of a car. Leila glanced quickly at the Uber sticker on the passenger side of the front windshield.

"Um, none?" Leila replied, grabbing the door handle. "Can you take me anyway? To Freeport? It's kind of an emergency. It's on Long—"

"South Shore, know it well," the driver said. "I mean, I don't mind, but you know that's a pretty long drive."

"I'll pay whatever you charge. Thank you!" Leila had never felt more thankful to her mom for giving her an emergency credit card. She pulled it out to show the driver, then yanked open the door and slid in the back seat. "Um . . . McNulty Street. I'm so grateful."

"Me, too. I can use the money."

Leila buckled her belt. The woman quickly tapped in the address to her GPS. She was wearing a knit cap. From beneath it, her hair spilled onto her shoulders. It was dyed a really pretty shade of blue.

2

Corey didn't expect to have prime rib and a biscuit for breakfast. But a guy next to the dumpster was sliding the meal toward him on a ripped piece of cardboard. He wore an old Mets baseball cap and clothes that looked three sizes too big. "Go ahead, it's yours," he said. "You seem hungry."

He was right. Corey felt a gnawing in his gut. The meat was half-eaten and turning green, and it looked like someone had sat on the biscuit. But the smell was way stronger than Corey expected and impossible to resist.

As he stepped toward it, saliva dripped from his mouth like a leaky bathtub faucet. It was embarrassing.

"Don't be afraid," the guy murmured. "Oh, hey,

sorry to be rude . . . I'm Chuck. Pleased to meet you."

Corey stepped closer.

The neon sign above them flickered the words "Baldwin Coach Diner." Corey knew Baldwin was somewhere near Freeport. He may have transspeciated, but he could still read.

He could also follow traffic signs. Those signs had led him down Sunrise Highway. The road was wide, and it was easy to evade humans. All he'd had to do was stick to the side near the elevated railroad tracks. No one walked there.

Now, as Corey sniffed the steak, insects scrambled out from beneath it. This was disgusting. He knew it was disgusting. But his jaw began attacking the meat as if it were the last day of his life.

Which it might have been.

When he looked up, Chuck was staring at him curiously. "What the heck are you, anyway, some kind of husky?"

Corey burped.

"I guess that's a yes?" Chuck said.

"Excuse me," Corey blurted. His voice sounded thick and deep. It would take a while to get used to it.

"*What the*—" Chuck scrambled to his feet.

"Rrrr . . . owooo," Corey moaned.

He cringed. That was a really bad attempt to make an animal noise. A transspeciated wolf should have been able to do better.

"Nooooo—no, you spoke! Like, words. I heard you. Or have I totally lost it?" Chuck leaned closer. "Go ahead. Seriously, say something."

Corey sighed. "Something."

"Gaaaaaahhhh!" Chuck yelled, jumping back. "Okay. This . . . it's like a prank, right? Some Bluetooth thing? You're gonna post this on social media and make me look like an idiot?" He turned and shouted into the parking lot. "*You people don't got nothing better to do? Yo! You can't use my image unless I sign a release!*"

The air was changing. Corey could sense the brink of dawn. He needed to run. "Um, can you tell me where One seventy-six McNulty Drive is?" he asked. "In Freeport."

Chuck whirled back to Corey. "You got no receiver. You got no collar to put the receiver on. You . . . you moved your lips. You actually—"

Corey bared his teeth and growled.

"Two blocks away, past the high school, right on B-B-Brookside, keep going— McNulty is near the canal!" Chuck blurted.

"Thank you." Corey eyed a half-eaten black-and-white cookie near Chuck's left foot. He lunged for it, gobbled it down, and sprinted back toward Sunrise Highway.

His paws padded quietly. His breaths made little puffs. It was colder out here than in the city. Honestly, this didn't seem like the kind of place where Papou would live. It was so . . . flat. Papou was a city person. He hated the suburbs. He hated the country even more. *I got all the country I need in Central Park*, he loved to say.

Boom. There it was—a high school on the right, just as Chuck said, followed by Brookside Avenue. Corey slipped under a ripped cyclone fence and took a shortcut across the baseball field. But a pickup truck was pulling to the curb in front of the school, the window rolling down. From inside the pickup, someone was taking his photo.

Corey reached the sidewalk in three leaps. But by the time he sprang for the phone, the window was sliding shut. His paws and snout bounced against the glass, he fell to the sidewalk, and the truck peeled away.

Oh, great. The last thing he needed was a social media mob. He'd have to be more careful.

The street was deserted now. Just past the school

was a pond, and beyond it a narrow park. A creek ran through the park, snaking behind the houses that faced Brookside.

Tall grass. Reeds. Perfect cover.

The park lawn felt soothing beneath his paws. A horned owl eyed him from a maple tree. In the creek a mallard flew away in a panic. A possum slinked into a hole. But no humans.

He reached McNulty Drive and headed left between houses. As he crossed Brookside, the neighborhood was dark except for an occasional porch light. After a block and a half, he stopped at a neat, white-shingled bungalow. Over the front door was a faded wooden carving of a bald eagle.

Its talons surrounded the number 176.

Corey stepped closer. He heard the first birdcall of the day, in the branches of a peely-bark tree. The air was becoming silvery, hinting at the sunrise to come. He'd have to do this fast.

In the living room of 176 McNulty, a light flicked on.

Corey padded up three cement steps, onto a small porch. He kept his eye on the wide picture window. Through a pair of sheer curtains he could see an old man in a flannel robe walk slowly across the room.

It was only a matter of seconds before the man sat

on a sofa and sank out of sight. But Corey had seen more than enough to recognize his *papou*.

A high-pitched whine escaped from Corey's throat. He couldn't help it. Moving closer, he scratched at the metal part of the front screen door. He put his weight into it, because behind the screen door was a second door, thick and wooden, which was shut tight. Sound would have to carry through both.

Out of the corner of his eyes Corey saw the old man through the glass again, still in the living room. Papou walked toward the front picture window, pulling the curtain aside.

Corey's body jerked back and forth. It took him a moment to realize why.

His tail was wagging.

He moved closer to the window, hoping to catch Papou's attention. But the old man's eyes were looking out over his head, toward the street. So Corey scratched harder.

A moment later the wooden front door opened.

The old man's face was framed with a gray beard, his feet clad in his favorite fuzzy L.L.Bean slippers. He looked the same as always. As if nothing had happened.

There was so much Corey wanted to say. About the time hop that forced his body to change. About his fears that his grandmother might be dead. But all that came out of his mouth were two words.

"Hi, Papou."

The old man jumped back. Quickly he reached into the drawer of a desk by the door. He pulled out a pepper-spray container, aiming straight at Corey's head.

3

"D on't!" Corey said, backing away slowly from the screen door. He tried to activate his smile muscles, but he knew that was probably useless. "It's me, Papou," he said quietly. "Corey. Your grandson."

Papou's face was drawn and bone white. Corey wanted to jump on him and lick his face, but he held back. Animal instincts had to be suppressed.

Corey knew the old man was shocked. Of course he was. Corey would be, too, if the roles were reversed.

"Don't be afraid," he said gently. "I know, I messed up. I—I transspeciated. But I guess that's kind of obvious, huh?"

"Gus?" a woman's voice called out.

Quickly Papou shoved the pepper-spray container into a desk drawer and slid it shut. A woman
appeared over his shoulder, walking briskly toward
him through the living room. She wore a gray skirt
and a loose-fitting white knit top over fuzzy brown
slippers. Her hair, which was pure white, looked wet
from a shower. "Gus?" she called out as she fastened
a pair of earrings. "Gus, who is it?"

Papou was shaking head to toe. "Stay back, Fiona!"

"Fiona?" Corey murmured. He had never heard
Papou say that name.

The woman paid no attention to Papou's command,
walking up beside him and peering over his shoulder.
"There's no one here, you silly old—"

Corey spotted the color of her eyes now—a bright
green. When they met his, they seemed to grow three
sizes. "What is that?" she cried out.

"A stray!" Papou blurted. "I think it belongs to the
Pugsley boy."

"Shoo! Get out of here! Ucch, these new low-life
neighbors . . ." Fiona cried out. Cupping her hand over
her mouth, she screamed into the street: "*Whose dog is
this? Take it away or I'm calling the police!*"

"*I'm not a*—" Corey insisted, as the inner wooden
door slammed shut. "Papou! Papouuuuuuu!"

His cry became a howl. He felt his jaw lifting upward. It echoed into the night, until Corey heard a window snap open across the street.

"Shut that thing up before I call the police!" a voice boomed out.

Corey cowered against the porch wall. He had no plan B, but he needed one, and fast.

His own chest was heaving. His eyes took in the neighborhood. A light flicked on in a house across the street. On Long Island people got up early for the train to NYC. Everyone would see him. The sun would be his worst enemy. In full daylight, no one would mistake him for a dog.

The creek was the best place to hide. There, he could slip into the reeds and bushes until it was dark again. Then he'd give this another try. By then, maybe the old guy would be calmer. He'd have time to think. It would sink in that his grandson had suffered the worst consequence of time travel. And he'd know what to do.

It wasn't much of a plan. But it was all Corey had.

As he headed for the porch steps, he turned for one last look. Papou and Fiona were watching through the window. She was still shouting something, waving Corey away with her hand.

Corey gave them a wave of his paw, then turned

and leaped onto the lawn.

The pavement seemed to glow. The air was gray and liquid. He couldn't actually see the sun, but he could tell it was just brushing the horizon.

As his paws hit the sidewalk, he took off down McNulty toward the park. McNulty ended in a T shape at Brookside. Houses lined the creek to the left and right. Corey could pass between them to reach the bushes and reeds.

But as he reached Brookside, tires squealed to his right. A car was speeding toward him. It slammed on its brakes, fishtailing. Corey leaped away.

The car jumped the curb. Corey darted to the left, eyes on the passage to the creek.

"Corey!"

His brain was playing tricks now. Someone was shouting, and it sounded like his own name.

"Corey, you numbskull, get back here!"

His pace faltered. He slipped on a patch of ice in front of a small, white-shingled house.

He knew that voice.

The car was straddling the curb, about half a block away. As the back door opened, Leila Sharp stepped out.

"So, do you hate me?" she asked.

"L-L-Leila?" Corey said.

"D-d-duh?" Leila replied. "Yes, Leila. You ran away. When I was trying to help you! Do you hate me that much?"

Corey hung his head. A whimper escaped from his throat. "No."

Leila ran to him and knelt by his side. She was crying but her eyes were angry. "Why did you do that? You could have gotten yourself killed! You know how lucky you are that I found you?"

"Sorry," Corey said. "You showed me my *papou*'s address, and I couldn't stop myself. I know, I was really dumb. I just—I visited him, Leila. Papou. I scared him."

Leila's face softened. "Did he remember you?"

"I don't know. He's so different now. He's married to some stranger. I tried to tell him who I was. But his wife came up behind him and kind of went nuts. So I don't know if he recognized me."

"Smig and Auntie Flora didn't remember you at all. I mentioned your name—nothing. No recognition."

"Wait, what? How can that be?"

"Because you never existed, Corey."

"But you remember me."

"I know! I have no idea why I remember you. I shouldn't. It goes against the rules of logic and genetics." Leila took off her jacket and wrapped it around him. "You must be cold."

"Rules? You're talking about rules?" Corey said. "Here's a rule—people can't change the past. But being a Throwback breaks that one. Here are some others: Animals can't talk. People can't transform into animals."

"Corey—"

"Rules are only rules because they explain what we see!" Corey insisted. "When we see something different, the rules have to be changed!"

"Okay, I get the point," Leila said. "So what should we do? Go back to Papou?"

Corey thought a moment. "Well, not if Fiona's there. That's a one-way ticket for me to the Museum of Mutants. You know him, Leila. Maybe you should talk to him."

"Well, he has a phone number that's public," Leila said. "I'll call it. I'll tell him I'm a time traveler, too. I'll ask to meet privately. Meanwhile, you can't be seen. We've been hearing local police reports, Corey. They're looking for you. They have a photo. In front of the high school. They think you're a coyote. They're worried you're going to attack babies."

"Some guy in a pickup took that shot. I couldn't bite his arm off in time," Corey said. "But I love babies."

"Let's get in the car. I told the driver you were an

escaped pet dog. A rare one that looked like a wolf. She's cool. I trust her. It was a long trip from Central Park, and she says she's not even going to charge me. She's an animal lover. Her name is Bee. I told her you were friendly. So just act the part. And don't speak!"

Corey nodded. "Arf, arf."

"That sucked," Leila said. Then, turning toward the car, she called out, "Bring the blanket!"

"Blanket?" Corey asked.

"To hide you."

Bee stepped out of the car, grabbed a blanket out of the back seat, and ran toward them. "Hi, big guy," she called out, eyeing Corey warily. "You're not going to bite me, are you, cutey pie?"

"I prefer meat that's dead," Corey replied.

"*Corey!*" Leila yelled.

Bee's mouth dropped open. "He . . . he . . . *talked*."

"Sorry," Corey said.

"Don't run away!" Leila said, taking Bee's arm. "Please stay with us. We need you. I can explain everything." She took a deep breath. "He's my best friend, and he is human. *Was*, I mean. But he traveled in time and did something really radical."

"Traveled in time . . ." Bee murmured.

"He stopped himself from being born," Leila went

on, "and then came back to the present."

Bee nodded numbly. "As one does," she said, "when one travels in time."

"So when he returned, his genes went crazy," Leila said. "There was no more Corey template. So they jolted into a new life-form . . . what you see now."

"A talking wolf," Bee said.

"I can probably sing, too," Corey volunteered.

Leila glared at him.

For a long time Bee just stared. Then she scratched her head and snickered. "This is like some incredibly awesome comedy act."

"Awesome?" Corey said dubiously. "As in, *awesome?* As in, you're not afraid? You don't think we're bonkers?"

"Of course you're bonkers," Bee replied with a shrug. "But I'm a New Yorker. I've seen everything. Bonkers is somewhere between the Bronx and Yonkers."

Without thinking, Corey leaped onto Bee and began licking her cheek.

She nearly fell to the street.

"Corey!" Leila said, taking Bee away from Corey. "Sorry, he's just getting used to being this way. Let's get him out of sight."

Bee stood, looking a little shaken. She pointed her remote at the car, and the trunk opened.

"What?" Corey cried out. "No! You wouldn't even think of stuffing me in there if I were human."

"He has a point," Leila remarked.

"The back seat, then," Bee said, racing to the car. "Quick!"

She opened the back door, and Corey settled onto the carpet, which felt new and plush. As Bee threw the blanket over him, he looked up. "Sorry for yelling at you. And thanks for not freaking out."

Bee nodded. Her eyes were dark and piercing. The hair peeking out from under her cap was dyed blue. As Corey watched her slide into the driver's seat, the fur along his spine felt funny. Cold.

There was something about her face, he thought. Something familiar.

Bee's eyes were fixed on the rearview mirror. "Uh-oh," she murmured. "Get under the blanket."

"Why?" Corey said.

"Just do it!" Leila blurted.

A police siren shrieked behind them. Corey whimpered, shoving his face as deeply under the blanket as he could.

Muttering under her breath, Bee started the car and then pulled over to the side of the road.

"The carpet tickles my snout!" Corey whispered.

"*Don't talk! Be doggy!*"

Corey heard footsteps approaching the car as Bee shut off the engine and rolled down her window. "Good morning, officer," she said.

Corey tried to make himself as small as possible in the darkness. He moved his head from one side to the other, trying to keep the carpet out of his snout.

"Morning," a deep voice replied. "Awfully early to be out driving."

"We're . . . on the early shift," Leila said.

"At the hospital," Bee piped up.

"At the Dunkin' Donuts," Leila said at the same time.

"Both," Bee said. "I drive her to the hospital, and then I go to Starbucks."

"Dunkin' Donuts," Leila corrected her. "It has better coffee."

"It does not!" Bee snapped.

The carpet felt like teeny little insects dancing around the rim of Corey's nostrils. He crinkled his snout and held his breath.

Now another cop was standing just outside the door.

"My partner and me, we have the same argument," she said.

"I," Corey grumbled. "My *partner and I.*"

"Excuse me?" the cop said.

"Aye!" Leila shot back. "Aye-aye! All the time! Argue is our middle name."

"Well, just be careful, wherever you're going. We have reports of a wild coyote in the area. Attacked someone outside the high school."

"What? Wow!" said Leila.

Corey cringed. She wasn't going to win an Oscar.

Now his snout was starting to drip. His eyes watered.

One of the cops was tapping the side of the car. "Okay, then, if you see anything suspicious, you two, don't hesitate to call nine-one-one, okay?"

"You bet!" Bee said.

"Okay!" Leila piped up.

"Have a great—"

"*AAAAAH-CHOOO!*"

Corey's sneeze echoed in the car. For a moment, no one said a word.

"Ah-choo!" Leila repeated unconvincingly. "It's that time of the year. Allergies."

"It's the winter," one of the cops said.

"That was from the back seat," said the other.

Corey started to shake.

"Ma'am?" came the voice of the first cop. "Would you two step out of the car and show me what is under that blanket?"

4

Corey held still. He shoved his paws under his snout, to avoid the fibers of the carpet as much as possible. He willed his sinuses to be quiet. And he pretended to be asleep. Chest in . . . chest out . . .

Bee reached around and lifted the blanket. Corey felt a sudden chill.

"Whoa," one of the cops remarked, "he's a big boy."

"Very big," the other said.

Bee laughed nervously. "He's tired, or he'd say hello."

Bite them, Corey's wolf brain screamed out. *Bite them and run like crazy!*

Don't be a fool, his human brain replied.

He hated being in the middle of an argument.

"This baby sure ain't no coyote," said Cop number 2.

"He could probably snack on coyotes," Cop number 1 said.

"Is it a husky?" Cop number 2 asked.

"Um, yup! A purebred . . . Baltic husky," Leila improvised. "We just took him on a run. In the park."

"Yeah, my brother does a night shift, too," said Cop number 1. "Takes his little Lhasa apso for a walk at four in the morning. Winters are brutal."

Now another sneeze was creeping through Corey's snout. But Leila and Bee were both talking, talking, talking with cops.

"Well, then, you best keep this puppy at your side, in case there is any trouble," Cop number 2 said, his voice growing distant. "And don't hesitate to call us if—"

"*AAAAAH*-CHOOO!"

The moment Corey sneezed, the ignition rumbled.

"Will do!" Bee said, as the car bolted from the curb a little too fast.

"Bye!" Leila called out. "Thanks!"

As Bee made a left turn, she let out a groan. "I thought I was going to die."

"That was so awkward!" Leila blurted. "*Baltic husky?*

I don't even know if there is such a thing. I made it up."

"They couldn't have believed you," Corey said. "Cops are not fools."

Bee's eyes were fixed on the rearview mirror. "I guess these two are. They're driving in the other direction. Woo-hoo!"

As Corey climbed onto the back seat, Leila smiled at him. "You did great, Corey."

"Except for the grammar lesson," Bee said.

"And the sneezing," Corey added.

"It's the carpet," Bee said. "I'll disinfect it for next time."

"No next time, ever," Leila said. "Corey will be Corey again, if it kills me."

"Thanks," Corey said. "That's reassuring."

The houses on McNulty were bathed in the dull amber glow of a rising sun. Many of the darkened windows were brightly lit now, and a couple of cars were backing out of driveways.

Bee slowed down as she approached Papou's house. "That's it," Corey said. "The one with the eagle over the door."

"I'll talk to him," Leila said. "You two stay here."

As Bee parked at the curb, Leila got out and walked

toward the porch. The house was ablaze with lights. Corey could see the lawn clearer now. It was trim, decorated with a small team of plastic animals that smiled out from the hedges—reindeer, bunny rabbit, turtle.

"Cute house," Bee said.

"The weird thing, my grandfather would never live in a place like this," Corey said. "He never liked cute stuff. He never liked the suburbs. He was a city guy."

He eyed her carefully, but to his relief, she nodded as if Corey were 100 percent human.

In a few moments, Leila was running back to the car. Behind her, Papou stood in the front doorway. He was smiling nervously. But still, smiling.

Corey felt his tail wagging again.

"Fiona went to work," Leila said, leaning into the car window. "Papou is alone. I told him you're a trans-speciated time traveler. He gets that. He's curious and he's willing to talk to you. But I can tell he feels a little weird about it. Let me carry you in the blanket, okay? We have to keep you out of the neighbors' sight."

"I'll wait here," Bee said. "None of my business."

"I'm heavy," Corey said.

"I'm strong," Leila replied.

Corey hated being lifted. He was half Leila's size,

and she could drop him any minute. But he held still as Leila brought him into the house.

She set him down in a small living room that smelled of coffee and oldness. It had a worn green carpet and a brown velvet sofa. The mantel over the brick fireplace was crammed with photos, and bookcases lined the walls. Newspapers covered the coffee table, including a New York Times Magazine open to a half-filled crossword puzzle. "You do those in pen," Corey said. "And you never miss one clue."

"Yes," Papou said.

As Leila sat, Corey's eyes wandered up to the photos on the mantel. "There's Dad," he said. "And Yiayia."

Papou was still standing, clutching the back of an armchair. "Excuse me?"

"It's a long story," Leila said. "He just transspeciated a few hours ago. It happened to my aunt Flora, too. She got nailed when she went into the past too many times to try to save someone's life. But Corey—"

"Flora Sharp?" Papou asked, shooting her a glance. "Oh, dear. She was in my Knickerbocker group. We all worried about her."

"She's a strange white cat-doggish creature now," Leila said. "You were lucky. It didn't happen to you.

Even though you also went back to the same period of time again and again."

Papou looked away. "Yes. Trying to save my dear first wife."

"Yiayia, who went to her office in the World Trade Center on nine-eleven," Corey murmured, turning to face his grandfather. "So you remarried, Papou, and you moved to a place like this?"

"Sixteen years ago in October." Papou cocked his head curiously. "What is this all about? Why are you calling me *papou*? *Panayia mou*, are you Gregory?"

"Who?" Corey said.

"His name is Corey," Leila said. "He didn't transspeciate because of the usual reasons. It was because he changed something in the past. He's a Throwback."

Papou narrowed his eyes. "A Throwback . . ."

"Doesn't exist, right?" Leila said. "I know. You were taught that's a legend, right? But it's not. Corey proves that."

Corey was barely listening to the conversation. His eyes were fixed on a wedding photo on the mantel. He recognized his dad in a tux. He'd seen his mom and dad's wedding picture a million times. But the bride in this photo was a total stranger.

Of course.

For a moment he couldn't breathe. If Mutti and Papi never met, then his mother hadn't been born either. So Dad had married someone else.

Which would explain all the photos of another stranger—a boy at different ages. There he was in a crib, in a Spider-Man costume, in a graduation gown. "The boy," Corey said softly. "Is that your grandson?"

Papou gently took down a photo and held it. "Brave, sweet Gregory. My *palikari*! The love of my life. We lost him two years ago. On a mountaineering trip. Thirteen years old, he was."

"That's so sad," Leila said.

"The worst part? I hadn't seen Gregory since he was nine. My son's wife, Francesca, pah. She did not like me. She heard me talking about time travel and she assumed I was a crazy man. A bad influence. They moved to Colorado and I wasn't invited to visit. He wrote me secretly. He had grown interested in the outdoors. I encouraged him to go on a mountaineering trip. Later, when they found out . . ." Papou's eyes were watering. "I—I never said good-bye to him. Never really knew him. And I never will. They didn't recover Gregory's body. All these years, in the back of my mind, I had the hope that he survived. I thought . . . maybe . . . you . . ."

Corey's brain felt like it was being stretched inside out. "I'm not Gregory, Papou, and I'm sorry about what happened. But you . . . you had another life, and all the details were different. I know this will be hard to understand, but everything was different before I transspeciated. Your son is my dad. He didn't marry Francesca. He married another woman, my mom. And she didn't think you were crazy. She loved you. We lived in an apartment in a brownstone on West Ninety-Fifth Street. You were always talking about your first wife, Maria. You never got over what happened to her during nine-eleven. When I discovered I was a Throwback, I went back to try to save her. But I was new to time-hopping. I slipped around in the past. I ended up in New York in 1917. I thought I really blew it, but time is weird. In the end, it worked out."

Now Papou's face was turning pale. "My Maria lived?"

"Yes," Corey said. "You'd been so sad for so many years, but when I came back, the sadness was gone. Because of what I did, she never even got that job in the World Trade Towers. So you never had to experience her loss. Everything was perfect. I should have left it there. But I got it in my head to do something big. I know it sounds dumb, but I thought I needed to."

Papou nodded. "To help the world," he said softly, "instead of just yourself and your family. Because with that superpower, you felt a responsibility."

"Exactly!" Corey said. "So Leila and I went back to try to stop Hitler."

"*Vre, paithi mou.*" Now Papou was doing the sign of the cross.

"Yeah, that didn't work out," Corey said. "But it gets worse. Something I did prevented my grandparents on my mom's side from ever meeting. And when I came back, I looked like . . . well, the way I am now."

Corey heard the doorbell ring. Out of the corner of his eye, he saw Leila opening the door. But his focus was on Papou. "You are the smartest man I know," Corey said. "We did puzzles together, you and me. Anagrams. You wrote to me in code all the time. You always said that *anything* can be solved. I believe that. I want to undo what I did, Papou."

"You . . . you want me to have a different life than the one I know," Papou said. "The life in New York City, with my wife, still alive, and a different daughter-in-law . . ."

"And me," Corey said meekly.

Now Leila came away from the door and took Papou's hand. "Do you have any contacts with the

Knickerbockers? Any insight about time travel? If we can figure this out, things will go back to where they were. When Corey changes the past, any memory of that past is gone. You can't remember things that didn't happen. You won't remember all the tragedies."

"I understand." Papou shuffled the papers on the coffee table, stacking them in a neat pile. "And I miss my Maria so very, very much."

"So you'll help us?" Corey said.

Papou leaned toward him. "I believe you. But you may be thinking of this the wrong way. What if, when a Throwback travels in time, he or she is not really changing time at all?"

"I've seen it happen, Papou," Corey protested.

"What if you're not seeing it right?" Papou said. "Many scholars—smart people—they saw time as a tree. In one reality, the batter hits a grand slam in the bottom of the ninth. In the other, he pops up. In one reality, President Kennedy is shot in 1963. In the other, Lee Harvey Oswald is distracted and never fires the rifle. Each of these things is equally likely to happen. What if they both do? The tree branches, again and again, each time a different thing happens. These separate realities, they all exist—all together. They go forward side by side, and they don't see each other. Maybe thousands or millions of them. So if we say that this is true, the idea of a Throwback is very different, no?"

"Wait. You're saying a Throwback's superpower isn't really to *change* time," Corey said, "but to go back and make a whole new branch?"

"Exactly, *bravo!*" Papou replied. "So this other reality you speak of—where your grandparents meet—maybe it still exists, somewhere. I don't know. My brain cannot solve this puzzle. The thing is, *paithi mou*, I only know one life. This one." He gestured around to the living room, the window. "Family is family. I loved my Gregory. He may be gone, but he is in my heart. I can't help you wipe that away."

"You loved me, too!" Corey pleaded.

"I'm sure I did," Papou said. "In another life. But I don't know you in this one, *paithi mou*. Do you understand? Maybe someone else can help you. Maybe the Knickerbockers. But I can't. I—I'm sorry."

"*I need you. You can't let me stay like—like—!*"

Corey's voice was deepening to a growl. He felt his neck stretching upward, his legs coiling.

"Corey . . ." Leila said. "Corey, what is happening to you?"

But Corey wasn't seeing a living room anymore. He was seeing a fiery pit of flames. An old man full of fear.

It was the fear that made his blood boil.

As he leaped for his grandfather, he couldn't hear the shocked scream.

All he could see was the pale expanse of his *papou's* throat.

5

The blow to Corey's neck felt like a rifle shot. He hurtled across the living room. His head banged into the bricks of the fireplace.

The taste of blood was on his tongue. His teeth had grazed the old man's skin. He coughed and tried to focus on the room.

Bee was facing him, holding a long, hooked metallic object. An andiron from the fireplace. Leila was kneeling next to Papou on the sofa, her arm around his shoulder. He was sprawled out, moaning and half-conscious.

"What did you do?" Bee screamed.

Corey wanted to attack her, too. For sneaking into

the house when she was supposed to be in the car. For hitting him so hard.

Why was she here?

Papou was bleeding now. Leila jammed a pillow against his neck, and the fabric was turning red.

"Papou . . ." Corey murmured.

He had done this. He hadn't meant to, but it had happened anyway. He'd lost control.

And as he glanced back at Bee, he was about to lose it again.

"Corey . . ." Leila was crying now, her eyes swollen with fear. "Corey, get out of here."

He didn't need any prompting.

As he leaped away, both Leila and Bee jumped back. He headed for the front door but veered away. His mind was a mess right now, but he knew he couldn't go outside. That would be too risky.

Instead he detoured farther into the house, through a dining room and a kitchen. There, a hallway led to a bright, spacious room. Corey jumped down three small steps into a kind of home entertainment area, with a big flat-screen TV and a couple of armchairs. Here he could hide. Gather himself.

He paced, trying to calm his thoughts. The bookcase

was full of kid stuff—trophies, diplomas, and games. Framed drawings hung on the walls. I LOVE YOU, POPOO—XOXOX, GREGORY, one of them said, written by some teacher in neat handwriting beneath some toddler scribble. Dusty toys were piled in a basket in the corner, and a set of ski poles rested against the bookcase.

It was a Gregory room, a shrine to the love of Papou's life. The boy who never existed, until Corey made him happen.

The boy who erased Corey from Papou's heart.

Corey didn't mean to howl, but he was doing a lot of things he didn't mean to do, and the sound ripped up from the bottom of his soul.

Footsteps tapped up the hallway, and then Leila stood in the door. "He's going to be okay," she said. "Your *papou*. Bee is talking to his doctor right now."

"Good. That's good."

"But I'm worried about you."

"Thanks. Thanks a lot." Corey was huffing and puffing now, walking in circles. "But I'm *not* okay. I can't control myself."

"We need to get you help, Corey."

"Oh, yeah, that's a great idea," Corey snarled. "I'll

talk to the doctor. Hello, sir, I'm a talking wolf? Yup, the one that mauled Mr. Fletcher. Can you give me a checkup?"

"This isn't like you, Corey. . . ."

"Oh, you noticed?" Corey said. "You're right, I'm not like me. But also, here's what I'm thinking. I'm not like Smig either, or your aunt. I don't want to hide and fart and live in the Central Park mud. Take me to the ASPCA and have them put me to sleep, okay? I'm not good for anything."

"That's not funny, Corey," Leila said. "You are scaring me."

Now Bee appeared behind her. "What's going on?"

"Corey's in trouble," Leila said. "I don't know what to do."

Bee nodded, her blue hair sweeping her shoulders. "Okay. Um, I know this will sound weird, but . . . that's what I'm here for."

Corey's legs locked.

The blue hair. The face. He knew where he'd seen her before.

He threw back his head and cackled. At least he wanted to cackle. It came out more like a deep, ugly bark. Ugly enough that both girls jumped back.

"Trilby," he said.

Bee's eyes fixed on his. She didn't say a word.

"That's your name, isn't it?" Corey continued. "'Bee' is short for 'Trilby'—trill, bee. The girl with the blue hair on the C train platform."

"Wait—what?" Leila said.

"The night my sister, Zenobia, was attacked on the subway," Corey said. "I went back in time, less than an hour, to stop the attacker. She was there—Bee—pretending to be a random person. On the TV news that night, there she was again. They interviewed her. She took all the credit."

Bee stepped in front of Leila now, grabbing a ski pole. Holding it tight. Her hands were shaking. "I can explain. But we need to go."

"You can try hitting me over the head with that pole," Corey said. "But it's really lightweight aluminum."

"I'm not going to do that," Bee said calmly.

"Well, stabbing won't work," Corey said. "That thing won't penetrate my supertough wolf hide."

"Now, Corey . . ." Bee said.

He hated her steadiness. He hated that she wouldn't tell him who she was. He hated everything about his life at that moment. "Well, maybe I could just shred it apart and eat it. Then those sharp sharp edges would tear open my stomach and I would be out of my misery."

"Corey, that's disgusting, stop it!" Leila shouted.

Corey sprang for the pole. His jaw clamped on the metal. He could hear Leila screaming. She was trying to pull it away. Bee held on tight, too, the three of them struggling for control.

Something jolted through Corey. As if the entire electrical grid had pumped through that ski pole.

His jaw locked. The metal seemed to be taking over his body. It flowed into his bloodstream like liquid, invaded the air with a smell so foul he didn't want to breathe.

And then everything vanished in an explosion.

6

The ski pole was frozen to Corey's tongue. And someone was pulling on it.

As he scrambled to his feet, snow blasted his face so hard it felt like sand. He realized he'd been unconscious. He cried out in pain, but "Stop it!" came out more like "Hnah ih . . . !"

Whoever was holding the pole let go. Corey couldn't see a thing, but his mouth instantly began to warm. Saliva flowed, and he held the pole tightly in his teeth, letting it loosen from his tongue.

From the angle he knew he was on a steep hill. He looked left and right, but the snow stung his eyes.

There. A grayish lump in the snow below him. Corey stepped downward toward the figure. He nuzzled it until it turned and moaned.

He saw a flash of blue hair.

Bee. Or Trilby. Or whatever her name was.

She was a time traveler, too.

Her face was nearly the same blue as her hair. Her waist-length peacoat wasn't nearly enough to keep her from freezing. Corey couldn't stand her. But seeing her like that was scary. He didn't want her to die. Corey lay himself over her for warmth. He tried as best as he could to shake her shoulders. "Bee! Bee, it's Corey!"

Bee's eyelids were caked with snow. Corey let out a warm breath to unfreeze them. With a sudden cough, she turned her head. "Uch, what did you have for lunch?"

Corey had to shout to be heard over the wind. "*Was that you pulling the ski pole from my mouth just now?*"

"No!" Bee shouted back.

"*Do you understand what just happened? We hopped in time!*"

"Yes!"

"*You've been a time traveler all along? You just didn't tell us?*"

"Yes. It's a long story."

"*Do you know where Leila is? She pulled me out. She should be right here!*"

"I don't know. I was unconscious." Bee squinted, looking around. "She must have fallen back. Stumbled.

I don't know. There's no visibility, Corey. You can get lost here in a nanosecond. *Leila?*"

Corey lifted his head and called, "Leila! *Leila where are you?*"

Now Bee was struggling to her elbows. "*LEI-LAAAA!*" she repeated.

As they fell silent, Corey thought he heard a muffled groan up the hill behind them. "What was that?"

"The wind?" Bee said.

"That didn't sound like wind. Can you walk?"

As Corey backed off Bee, she staggered to her feet and shook herself off. "I'm f-f-f-fine."

"You're freezing," Corey replied. "Follow me."

Corey put his head down. Fighting the wind, he trudged through the snow up the incline. It only took three or four steps before he nearly fell over another lump under the snow. "Bee, help me here!" he said.

Together they lifted an inert body from the snow, dressed in a thick down parka. A wool cap—a balaclava—covered the whole face. "Not Leila," Corey said.

"Hey! Hey, wake up!" Bee shouted.

Now Corey heard the groan again. This time it was closer, just a few feet to the left. And it was definitely Leila's voice.

The wind was picking up now, whistling. Corey fought to keep straight, but the groaning had stopped. In the distance he heard a crack. He stopped walking.

The ground began to shake. An eerie, low sound rumbled from above them. It quickly grew to a dull roar, until it was loud enough to muzzle the shriek of the wind.

"What is that?" Bee's voice cried out.

"I think," Corey shouted back, "it was an avalanche."

"*Was?*"

Corey braced himself. The sound was growing softer, but it still felt as if a subway were running underneath them. Now he could hear the wind's howl again.

"A minor avalanche," Corey said. "We're okay."

He called Leila's name again until the ground began to move. Again.

This time the movement was not a vibration. It was a slide. The white expanse was dropping downward, folding in on itself. It was picking up speed, disappearing like water down a drain.

Corey turned away from the sinking snow. But the collapse was growing outward. He sank too, facing a slope that grew steeper by the second. Digging his paws into the snow, he tried to haul himself upward, toward the peak of the collapsing snow. But the motion was making his body slide downward with the pull of gravity.

A yawning pit opened beneath him, black and bottomless.

And he screamed.

"Beeeeeee!" Corey shouted.

His voice was dry and muffled, swallowed up by the void. Planting his haunches, he flung himself upward. As his paws plunged into the snow, he pulled up his legs beneath him and leaped again.

But he was losing ground, sinking downward. The top of the crevasse was getting farther away, not closer. With each thrust, the snow slid out from under him. He was all instinct now, muscle and sinew. He forced his body upward, faster and faster, trying to keep pace against the pull of the snow. Commanding himself not to look down, not to look down . . .

The blizzard pounded from above, blurring his sight. A broken-off branch smacked his shoulder. Rocks pelted his back. When something hard hit him square on the head, he ignored it like all the other debris. Until he saw what it was.

The end of a rope, swinging before his face.

As he clenched it between his teeth, his paws gave way and he dropped.

The rope went taut. The force of his weight nearly yanked the teeth from his head. He was hanging now, his legs pedaling wildly, his jaw gripping the rope like a vise. Through the wind's shriek, he heard a scream.

The rope pulled him upward. He worked his paws against the snow, trying to add to the momentum. The top of the crevasse was closer now. He was rising, but his jaw felt as if it were coming loose in his head. The rope shredded against the sharpness of his teeth, coming apart strand by strand. The ripped fragments felt like a wire brush against the inside of his mouth. Now the center of the cord was thin as a string, but he couldn't loosen up or he would drop.

He dug harder, until the rope snapped in two.

"Gotcha!"

A hand closed around his left paw and clenched tight. Corey hung suspended over the blackness for a moment, and then he felt himself rising.

As he reached the top of the crevasse he came eye

to eye with a face covered in a balaclava. It was the figure he'd found unconscious in the snow, the nearly dead stranger. He was definitely alive now, and flat on his stomach. Behind him, flat on hers, Leila was holding his ankles. And behind her, Bee completed the human chain.

The stranger yanked hard, and Corey shook himself loose. His paws had purchase now, and he ran away from the crevasse. The others scrambled to their feet and followed. He could see a grove of pine trees in the swirling whiteness. It was a place where there might be some protection from the wind.

Corey reached it first. Under the tree canopies, the snow was deep but the wind was calmer. At the base of a thick-trunked pine, he paused and looked back. Through the warm clouds of breath, he spotted the others.

"*Coreeeeey!*" Leila screamed happily, nearly falling on top of him.

Against his better judgment, he began licking her face. "Sorry," he said, his jaw aching with each syllable, "I can't stop myself. I thought you were lost."

"B-B-B-Bee found me. I was holding the p-p-pole. Then I wasn't. There are rocks. Under the s-s-snow. I fell and hit my head."

It was great to be alive, and to see Leila. But her body was shaking. Her lips were nearly blue. Her jeans jacket was no protection against this kind of cold. She and Bee wouldn't be able to survive here much longer, dressed as lightly as they were. "We have to get out of here," Corey said.

"Ho. Ly. Crap." The not-dead stranger was staring at Corey with eyes as white as the snow. He was not that much older than Corey.

"I get that response a lot," Corey said. "But thanks. For pulling me out."

"Um. Um." The guy gulped, looking helplessly at Bee, then Leila, then Corey again. "You're welcome?"

"It's a l-l-long s-s-story," Leila said, shivering.

"But she can't tell it if we die here," Corey added. "Do you know the area?"

The guy nodded. He pulled off a thick ski glove and reached into his pocket, pulling out a handheld device about twice the size of an iPhone. "Hang on . . . this is a dedicated GPS device. Better than a phone."

As the kid stared at it, Corey noticed his lips were purple. So were Bee's. They didn't have much time.

"Okay. Okay," he said. "I got separated from my group. . . . Okay. I see where base camp is. We shouldn't be too far. Follow me."

"Let me take you," Corey said to Leila.

"What?" she replied.

"Lie on my back."

"What are you talking about?"

"Lie on my back," Corey repeated. "I'm warm. Well, warmer than you. I can carry you. It'll be awkward, but you can die of exposure."

"Do it," Bee said. "And if you warm up, maybe I can take a turn."

The other guy was staring at them all. He knocked himself lightly on the head. "I don't know which part of this is real and which is a hallucination. But I don't care. Follow me."

He turned his back and began to walk. Leila draped herself over Corey's back, holding tight to his chest. Then she lifted her legs and crossed them above her back.

"You're right," she said. "This is awkward."

It felt like hours before Corey spotted the outline of a structure in the distance. It wasn't much larger than a hut. A metal pipe protruded from the roof, sending up a curl of gray smoke. By that time the snowfall had eased. Bee was draped on his back now, and Leila walked arm in arm with the stranger.

As the hut came in sight, the door flew open. A bearded man stood, gaping for a second. He was dressed in a thick wool sweater, sturdy boots, and a peaked wool cap, and he burst toward them at a run.

"Fletcher!" he cried out. "Haaa! Ha ha ha! What a sight for sore eyes!"

Corey stopped for a moment. "Wait. How does he know who I am?" he murmured.

"What the—?" Leila added.

But the older man wasn't looking at Corey. He reached the young stranger first and wrapped him in a hug.

"Sorry, Mr. Rogers," the kid replied. "I messed up. I went off from the group, and then the blizzard started."

While the two talked, Bee climbed off Corey. "I'm going in. Join me."

As she and Leila ran for the door, the man named Rogers seemed to notice them for the first time. "Dear lord, where did they come from?" he said, following them into the hut. "Come in, come in, let me get you some blankets and some hot cocoa!"

The kid turned toward Corey and took off his balaclava. "You, too, my friend," he said, gesturing toward the hut. "Come in."

Corey got a good, undistracted look at his face. He

recognized the features now. The kid was smiling. It was the same smile that had beamed from a photo fresh in Corey's memory.

The graduation photo on Papou's mantel.

"What are you waiting for?" bellowed Rogers from within the hut. "And for goodness sake, shut that door, Gregory!"

8

"How I can repay you?" said Gregory Fletcher. "If you hadn't found me, I would have died."

Bee and Leila were shivering under thick plaid blankets, nursing cups of hot cocoa at a small table by a potbellied stove. "Hot chocolate is f-f-fine," Leila replied.

Corey eyed Gregory. Gregory, the replacement grandson.

The guy had a friendly face. He was tall, like Corey was. His voice was high and a little squeaky, like Corey's. His hair was lighter. It didn't rise up from his head like a bush, the way Corey's used to. He was a little older. He was like Corey, only perfected.

"I got through to the others. They're on their way,"

Rogers said, looking up from a phone. As he pocketed it, he caught a glimpse of Corey for the first time. "Whoa. What's that doing here?"

"He saved our lives, Rogers," Gregory said. "He deserves some respect."

"He's a wild animal, Gregory!" Rogers replied.

"He sure doesn't behave like one," Gregory said. "Look at him."

Soaking up the warmth of the stove, Corey closed his eyes and let out a very cute-sounding "Hrrmmmm."

"You said 'others,' sir?" Bee quickly asked.

"There are fifteen of us," Rogers replied, warily watching Corey. "And three guides. ASAG. The Arctic Survival Adventure Group. We've been doing this for two decades and never lost anyone. I—I confess I'm a little shell-shocked. We weren't expecting this blizzard. The forecast was clear and sunny."

"Okay, so what the heck were you guys doing here?" Gregory asked. "Dressed like *that*?"

Corey shifted on the floor, and Bee shot him a look that said *Don't speak.* He was fine with that. He had no urge to say a word. His jaw ached like crazy from the rope pull. And he could tell Rogers wanted to throw him out of the hut.

Besides, there was a lot to think about. Like what Papou had said about Gregory's death.

Gregory had been lost in a mountaineering trip. They hadn't found his body, just the ski poles. And how is a body "not found"?

If it disappears. And how does a body disappear on a mountain?

If it gets buried under snow. In an avalanche or down a crevasse, for example.

Corey had found Gregory buried in the snow after a blizzard. If he hadn't found him, Gregory might have stayed there. Or picked himself up and gotten sucked into the crevasse.

Again Corey had changed history. Saved Gregory's life. And in the weirdest twist, Gregory had saved his, too.

Corey knew he should feel happy. Gregory didn't die, and so his *papou* would never know the grief of losing his grandson. That was a good thing. A miracle!

But all he felt was emptiness. He hadn't meant to go back into the past. He hadn't meant to do any of this.

Gregory was asking a lot of questions now, the way Corey would. "So, how did you guys end up here? Not to be judgy, but you're so totally not dressed for the weather."

"Car accident," Bee lied. "We sped out. Toward . . . a cliff. We had to hop out. In our car clothes."

The older man cocked his head. "Wow. The road is nearly four miles away."

"They're tough, Rogers," Gregory said with a laugh. "And I'll be grateful the rest of my life."

"Well, we're grateful to *you*," Leila said. "You saved Corey."

"We *all* saved him," Gregory said.

"*Corey?*" the man named Rogers asked.

"That's, um, the name we gave the . . . husky," Bee quickly said.

"Who found Gregory," Leila added. "And saved his life."

Now Rogers was cautiously walking toward Corey, his eyes narrowed. "That doesn't look like a husky."

"He's Baltic," Bee said. "A special breed. Looks just like a wolf."

"Hm. Baltic husky. Never heard of that." Rogers was reaching into a pack, slipping something into his pocket. Corey didn't know what it was, but he could sense it was something for protection. Something that could hurt Corey.

He felt the hairs on his back bristle. When he was a human, he had learned that animals sensed fear. Now he knew what that sense was like. Fear was weakness, but weakness was threatening. A person who felt weak could attack. Rogers was full of fear. It projected toward Corey like an electric jolt, as strong and sudden as if he'd stuck his finger in a socket. It left a bitter, metallic taste in his mouth.

A sudden growl from somewhere in the room startled him, until he realized it was his own.

"Guys . . ." Bee said. "I think we have to go."

Now Gregory was eyeing the older man. "Rogers, the husky—Corey—he's friendly. Without him, I wouldn't be here."

Corey wanted the man to back off. To lose his fear. But Rogers wasn't moving.

The muscles in Corey's face were acting on their own, pulling his lips back from his teeth. His legs coiled underneath him, ready to spring.

"He doesn't look friendly to me," Rogers said.

"Corey . . ." Leila said, walking toward him. "Corey, it's okay."

"I think," Corey growled, "it's time."

At the sound of Corey's voice, Rogers screamed. As he fell back onto a chair, the door to the hut opened. A group of ice-caked explorers stood there, staring at the scene from behind fur-trimmed hoods.

But Corey saw it only for a moment, before Leila and Bee jumped on him.

9

This time, he didn't think he'd make it.

He saw his arms stretch into space like rubber. His own howls came from miles away. He felt his head separate from his neck, then split in half and then in half again until it was in fragments. Was this real? It couldn't be real. But the pain was intense, then unbearable, then the size of the entire universe.

And when it stopped, he couldn't see a thing for a good five minutes. "Ohhh," he groaned. "Why do we do this?"

Leila's voice broke the silence. "Corey? Are you okay?"

"I don't know," he said. "Do I have a snout?"

No answer meant yes.

He shook himself and stood. He was on all fours. Which wasn't a good sign either. "I feel sick," he said. "I think I'm going to barf."

Leila and Bee slowly came into focus. They didn't look all that great either. Leila's hair was a sweaty tangle, and Bee seemed nauseated, too. "Don't barf," she said. "Because if you do, I will, too."

As Corey's vision came back, he realized they weren't where they'd started. Papou's den had been full of trophies, books, photos, and mementos.

The room they were in now was the same shape. With the same view. But it was empty.

Leila peered outside the door into the hallway. "What happened here? This is a ghost house."

Corey and Bee followed. The nausea was gone now, replaced by confusion. Their footsteps echoed as they passed down the hallway, through the kitchen, into the dining room, and then the living room. "Everything empty," Corey said.

"Maybe we came back to a different date," Leila suggested. "Like, a couple of years before Papou moved in here?"

Bee looked at her phone. "Nope. Same day we left, same year."

"Everything should be the same," Leila remarked. "What's up with that?"

"What's up," Bee said, "is that Corey changed history. And when that happens, nothing is predictable."

Corey stared at the blue-haired girl. So much about her was a mystery. "Who are you, anyway? Why were you in that subway? Why did you pick up Leila in that car, with a fake name? How can you know how to time-hop?"

"Okay, one question at a time." Bee smiled and took a deep breath. "Bee has been my nickname all my life. I'm a member of the Knickerbockers. I am what's called a Tracker. I seek out other time travelers."

"Who told you about us?" Leila asked.

Bee shrugged and turned away.

"Smig," Corey said under his breath. "And Catsquatch—Leila's Aunt Flora. Right? It had to be them. They're spies."

"Not spies, exactly," Bee said. "The KB—Knickerbockers—it's a friendly, supportive organization."

"Then why didn't you tell me on the way out here?" Leila asked.

"I wanted to wait until we had Corey," Bee said. "And then tell you both. Look, you need to know that everyone is *ecstatic* Corey exists. The KB needs him! An actual Throwback—someone who can change the past?—it's the holy grail of time travel."

"Sweet. Do I get a trophy?" Corey looked around the empty room. "Do I get the Knickerbockers to come here and explain what happened to my grandfather?"

"We can guess." Bee shrugged. "Before we left, your *papou* was estranged from his family, right? He was the one that encouraged Gregory's parents to send Gregory on the mountaineering trip. They blamed him for the death. So no death, no blame. No rift in the relationship."

"Maybe Papou doesn't live here," Leila said. "Maybe he lives closer to wherever Gregory's family lives."

"We can try to find your grandfather together," Bee said. "But now that Gregory's alive, Papou would be even *less* likely to help you."

"I know that," Corey said.

"There has to be another way to solve this problem," Bee offered.

"We can go back in time again," Leila said. "We just need to find the right moment."

"No. . . . No. Going into the past hurts more when you're an animal," Corey said. "I don't know why. Maybe it's the way transspeciating messes with your guts. I don't want to keep doing this. I don't want to keep going into the past and coming back exactly the same—or worse."

"You can't give up!" Leila said.

Corey shook his head. "You know what else? I hate being indoors. Part of me wants to just get outside and run and run and run. Maybe I'll end up in Canada and meet other wolves. Eat raw meat the rest of my life and sleep outdoors."

Corey eyed the door. The walls of the empty room felt like they were closing around him.

Now he felt Leila's hand on his shoulder. "Corey, stop this. You're not going out there in broad daylight."

Before he could decide what to do, he heard a noise from inside the house. The front door was opening.

Leila pulled him back. She put her finger to her lips.

Bee dropped to her knees. She quickly crawled to the far side of the living room, peeking through the sheer curtains. Her eyes widening, she waved them away from the door. "Hide!" she whispered.

Reluctantly Corey followed Leila and Bee to the den, where they crammed into an empty coat closet.

"Who is it?" Leila whispered.

"The wife," she whispered back. "Fanny?"

"Fiona," Corey grunted.

"What's she doing here?" Leila asked.

"Who cares?" Corey said.

"They're practically whispering," Leila said. "Which is weird in an empty house."

Bee began to pull the door shut, but left it open a crack. "I want to hear them," she said softly.

Voices murmured from the front room, subdued and serious sounding. As the sound of footsteps moved into the kitchen, Corey recognized Fiona's voice. He'd heard her through the screen door when he first saw Papou. But the other was a deep male voice he didn't know.

"We spent many wonderful years here," Fiona was saying. "Our grandson had a room of his own, full of light, perfect for a playroom and close to the kitchen. Feel free to look at any of the rooms."

They were coming closer now. Bee silently closed the closet door. Corey held his breath as the footsteps entered the den.

A sharp knock made him jump.

"Good walls," said the male voice, knocking again a little farther away. "Solid construction. That'll make this attractive to buyers. I don't think your house will be on the market for long, Mrs. Fletcher."

The sound of that name make Corey flinch. What kind of name was Fiona Fletcher anyway? Leila was holding him tight, but he had no desire to see the stranger Papou married.

"I won't be here much longer," Fiona said. "I'm flying back to my stepson's place on Friday."

The man chuckled. "Not to worry. Our firm will handle all the showings and report to you if anyone is interested. That's what we've been doing in this fine neighborhood for fifty years!"

Showings?

Corey realized this was a real estate agent. He wanted to show the house to possible buyers. Which meant Papou's wife was selling the place.

"You know, I'm sad to leave, but I'm glad some other family will be enjoying the place where Gus and I were so happy," Fiona said. "The one thing I worry about, Mr. Gormley, is the collection of boxes in the basement. My husband's things. They will be there for another week before the shipping company takes them."

"No worries. I will make sure no one touches them," said Mr. Gormley. "So then, if we have a contract, I'll just ask you to sign some papers?"

"Of course," Fiona said.

As the footsteps retreated toward the kitchen, Corey breathed a sigh of relief. He nodded toward Bee, and again she pushed the door open a crack.

"Oh, one thing," Mr. Gormley was saying. "About your husband. Gus."

Corey froze.

"Yes?" Fiona said.

"Forgive me if this sounds rude," Mr. Gormley said. "But home buyers can be a . . . well, a superstitious lot. If, for example, they hear a rumor about, say, a ghost—"

Fiona laughed. "There were no ghosts here."

"Or something, say, *tragic* happening in the house," Mr. Gormley went on. "Well, you know . . ."

For a long time Fiona was silent.

When Gormley spoke again, his voice was barely audible. "I'm . . . I'm so sorry. I didn't mean to upset you, but—"

"He . . ." Fiona sniffled. "He was inches from the driveway. He'd taken that trip to LaGuardia Airport a hundred times, dropping off Gregory. And that maniac in the motorcycle . . . Gus had to swerve, to avoid a collision. I didn't think he was going that fast. But he nearly took down that sycamore tree. And then . . ."

Her words choked in her throat.

"I'm so sorry for bringing this up," Gormley said. "I know how painful it must be."

"I called nine-one-one right away," Fiona went on. "But it was so cold outside, so I brought him in. I shouldn't have moved him. That's what did it."

"Of course . . . of course. You were just being compassionate. How were you to know? I'm just saying, in terms of our presentation . . ."

"Presentation?"

"What we tell the prospective buyers."

"I see," Fiona said, her voice sharpening. "You're saying, don't tell anyone a human died in this house. Because it may keep someone from purchasing it."

"It . . . it's just a recommendation," Gormley said. "People have superstitions."

The new reality hit Corey like the back of a shovel. Papou was gone. If Corey hadn't saved Gregory, Gregory wouldn't have visited. Papou wouldn't have had to drop him off at the airport. Papou would be home. Here. Alive.

He'd done it again. Messed up everything.

Enough.

He'd time traveled enough. Every single trip into the past had ruined things. They called it the butterfly effect. Step on a butterfly in the past and the future is changed forever. But that wasn't the right name. Not exactly.

Throwback curse was more like it.

That last trip to the Yukon, or wherever they were—that was it. No more.

No matter what happened, Corey Fletcher would never go into the past again. He didn't care who saw him or heard him. He didn't care what happened to him at all.

A cry welled up from deep within him. And Leila clamped both hands around his mouth.

PART II

Leila

10

I hate 2 write when the car is moving.

But I have to. This is why I keep you in my pocket. And I've been neglecting you 2 LONG!!!

If I get sick + puke all over this book, my fault. Bee just gave me the 👁 in the rearview mirror. She says she hasn't seen anyone actually WRITE BY HAND in a diary in about 10 years. I said 2 her, sorry 2 break yr record. She thought that was funny.

She has a very low bar for humor.

But more about her later.

I'm sick over what happened 2 ~~popou papoo~~ Corey's grandfather. Sick. I can't stop crying. But I'm more worried about Corey.

I think he's given up.

He nearly gave away our hiding place in that closet. P's wife was there with a real estate guy. We were lucky they were arguing so loud.

We were sooo lucky.

Anyway, we try 2 cheer up C and keep him positive. But EVERYTHING out of his mouth is nasty + sarcastic.

And then sometimes his eyes kind of go glassy. He just says yes + goes where we point him. And sleeps a lot. It's like he's lost all his willpower.

I mean, I don't blame him for the attitude. I really don't. What happened 2 him is crazy. If I were in his shoes, I don't know what I'd do.

He needs a shrink soooo badly. I would send him 2 mine if I didn't think she would run out of the apartment shrieking.

For example, on the way out of the house toward B's car, he's all wrapped up in a blanket so no one sees him. And guess what, he has 2 go 2 the bathroom. I figure, ooookkkk, bad timing, but he's a wolf, right, so we can bring him around back + he can go in the yard.

But he's like, I need 2 use. The. Actual. BATHROOM. Like what, he's 2 embarrassed for us 2 see him? I'm thinking, when he goes in there how is he even going 2 manage a toilet???

Ucch, that sounds like I'm making fun of him. I'm not. That's just an example of how he's losing a grip.

HOW ON EARTH DO WE GET COREY BACK?

Which brings me 2 Bee. Or Trilby. Bee the Knickerbocker who calls herself a Tracker. I figure it just means like a bounty hunter for time travelers. But she makes it seem like it's this big thing, a special talent like Throwbackery, or whatever you call it. But she won't really go into detail. She changes the subject.

Anyway, a few minutes ago we're zooming on the So. State Parkway and Bee says 2 Corey, why not just go back? Like, try 2 undo what you did in Germany. Instead of interfering with yr great-uncle, just hang back and let things happen the way they had before.

WHICH MAKES SENSE!

But not 2 Corey, who's, like, I already went back 2 that time, when I was a human! If I go again, as a wolf, I'll see myself!

So Wolf-Corey will see Human-Corey, Bee says. So you drag Human-Corey into the woods or something. Explain what's happening. Then you won't change history, yr grandparents can meet, and everything goes back 2 normal. She says the Knickerbockers will help "supervise" the trip.

Like it's a school field trip.

Well, I thought C was going 2 bite her head off. Literally! He's like, You want me 2 let my great-uncle be shot 2 death? You want me 2 be a murderer? I already just killed my grandfather!

We try 2 tell him that wasn't his fault. But he just digs in. After screaming and yelling for a few minutes he declares his time traveling days r done.

I just can't, he says.

Just can't. Just can't.

Over and over and over, until he's asleep and snoring.

I guess we're going 2 meet the Knickerbockers. So we'll see about "can't."

I'm kinda scared, but maybe they'll have some answers.

I can tell B's really upset. She's on the phone with the KB now. Talking about Corey in all this scientific lingo I don't understand.

+ Mom is texting me nonstop.

I don't know how I'm going 2 face her. She saw Corey. Well, she saw me taking a wolf out of the house. Since then I haven't been home. I keep texting her 2 say I'm okay. I made up some dumb excuse about a class animal rescue project and I love huskies. She was hysterical. But now I think she's better cuz she knows I'm alive + texting.

Still. It would be nice 2 know exactly WHERE we're going.

B won't tell me. I just have 2 trust her, she sez.

I want 2. She's smart and she wants 2 help. She helped me save C's life. But there's something so sneaky going on. On THE WHOLE DRIVE 2 Freeport B didn't tell me her real name. Or that she was stalking me.

So . . . should I trust her? Is there something else she's not saying?

Did I say I'm nervous? I'm nervous. Like, who r these KBs anyway? I always pictured some old white-haired types with George Washington hair drinking hot chocolate + talking bout the good old days, ho ho ho. Now I'm thinking bad guys with twirly mustaches.

It will b fine. Nothing can be worse than what has already happened.

I need 2 chill.

I need 2 get a life.

11

The traffic was thick on 110th Street, with both cars and people. Bee hit a red light on First, Second, Third, Lexington, and now Park Avenue. Leila's fingers drummed on her notebook as an Amtrak train raced north overhead, on tracks supported by an ancient-looking stone archway.

"Will you stop that?" Corey growled.

"Stop what?" Leila asked.

"That banging."

Corey had awakened somewhere on the RFK Bridge. Leila was hoping Corey's sleep would do him some good, but he was sour and cranky.

Leila herself had been down this street a hundred times in a bus and taxi, but she'd never felt this nervous in her own city. "How close are we to Knickerbocker headquarters?"

"I'm sorry," Bee said, "but we have to keep the location a secret. I'm not allowed to mention it even verbally. You'll have to trust me. We're heading to meet people who can help you."

"I told you, I am never, ever ever traveling into the past again," Corey shot back. "I can't."

"Yes, you've said that a hundred times already," Leila reminded him.

"Having you undo the past is not the only option," Bee said. "Look, I spoke to them while you were sleeping. They know everything about time travel. They want to see you. A Throwback is a miracle. They want to help you be human again. And they're geniuses."

"Whatever," Corey grumbled.

"Don't you want to be human again, Corey?" Leila asked.

"Um, yes?" Corey said. "Roadkill gets me all excited. I have this urge to eat birds. I see a squirrel, and I want to jump out the window and run after it. So if the Knickerbockers can go, poof, you're a human, great. If not, then please drive me to the woods and let me be miserable all by myself."

"You are so weird," Leila grumbled.

The car fell silent as the light turned green. In a few blocks Bee sped around a traffic circle at Fifth Avenue. Now Central Park was on the left. The slanted slate roof of the Harlem Meer discovery center rose over a peaceful lake. Leila could feel the temperature drop about five degrees.

Bee pulled the car to the right, screeching to a stop at the curb. An older white guy in an olive-green park ranger uniform stood against the wall of a brick building. He was about six foot four with droopy eyes, a thick white mustache, and a baseball-style cap. At the sound of Bee's horn, he threw a lit cigarette to the sidewalk and lumbered toward the car.

His eyes popped at the sight of Corey. "Good grief, this is the Throwback? This job isn't going to be easy."

"Nice to meet you, too," Corey said.

The guy took off his cap. Under it was a shiny bald head, which he wiped nervously. "Sorry, Wolfy. My name is Philbert."

"No worries, Baldy. My name is Corey."

Leila nudged Corey with her elbow. "Be nice," she whispered.

Bee shut the ignition and climbed out. "Phil, meet

Leila Sharp. Her aunt is a TS, too. The one we call Catsquatch."

"Wait, what's a TS?" Leila said.

"TS is a transspeciate," Philbert explained. "W-U-A-L-O-A. We use a lot of acronyms. See what I did there? We use . . . W, U? Haw haw haw!"

As he ran around the car to open the door, Corey gave Bee a look.

"He's a nerd, but you get used to him," Bee whispered over her shoulder.

Philbert opened the door. He reached in with a collar and a leash, which Corey batted aside. "What the—why are you doing this?" Corey demanded.

The old guy pointed to sign at the park entrance:

ALL DOGS MUST BE LEASHED

"I'm not a dog," Corey said.

"People will think you are," Philbert replied. "Most New Yorkers don't know a German shepherd from a German chocolate cake. Also, please don't talk. Or I will be forced to pretend I am a ventriloquist, and everyone will think you're a dummy. HAW haw!"

"Hilarious." Corey growled as Philbert put the

collar around his neck. At a break in the traffic, they all headed across. Philbert held tight to the leash as they walked quickly toward the entrance at Adam Clayton Powell Jr. Boulevard. Each of the park's entry gates had a name, and Leila couldn't help noticing this one was Warriors' Gate.

Leila kept her eyes straight ahead. She heard a dog growling to her left, and Corey bared his teeth at it. A squirrel raced by, and Philbert had to pull hard to keep Corey from chasing it.

On the other side of the park's main road they climbed a set of crude steps carved into a granite boulder. Sharp rocks bulged out of the ground, and trees reached stiffly to the gray sky.

At the top of the hill, nearly hidden by the trees, was a crude-looking building about the size of a public bathroom. It was built of stones that looked like they'd been cemented together in a hurry, hundreds of years ago. If there had been any roof, it was long gone. Small windows on each wall had been fitted with metal bars like a jail. On the south side, seven steps led up to a locked, rusted door. A lonely-looking American flag flapped in the breeze on a pole.

"The old blockhouse," Philbert said softly, reaching into his pocket. "Built to protect New York from the British during the War of 1812. Cannons used to point through these windows—north toward the valley, east toward the river, in case of attack. Back then, there were no trees blocking the view. They'd been cut down."

"I've been by this place a hundred times," Corey said. "This dump is the headquarters?"

"Not quite." Philbert looked silently in all directions, fingers to his lips. Satisfied the coast was clear, he scampered up the steps to the battered old metal door in the side of the blockhouse. It looked like the entrance to an ancient dungeon. Pulling what looked like a credit card from his pocket, Philbert tapped it to an old rusty lock.

It fell open with a solid thunk and he leaned into the door with his shoulder.

Groaning heavily, the door swung open. Inside the little fortress was a cement floor. It was cracked, dusty, and marked with tiny pools of black water. A startled mouse scurried into a hole at the opposite side, and weeds peeked out of crevices in the floor and walls.

Philbert walked to a spot at the dead center of the floor. Nothing seemed remarkable about it, but Philbert gestured toward them to stay clear.

He pointed his little credit-card gizmo downward.

A low rumble shook the building, and pebbles began to swirl on the floor.

Slowly, a perfect square at the center began to drop downward. It stopped a few feet below the surface, slid to the right, and tucked itself under the floor.

It left a hole of solid blackness.

Philbert smiled. He unleashed Corey.

"Welcome," he said, "to our headquarters."

12

Bee went first, stepping down a ladder. Leila knelt, trying to see what was down there. It was like a sewer—dark, humid, and smelly. "Are you sure there are no alligators down here?" she asked.

"Ha ha," Bee called upward. Now she was shining her phone flashlight around, walking on a dirt floor. Finally she flipped a switch on the wall. The fluorescent light gave the area a greenish-gray glow.

Leila took the wooden ladder slowly. It was warped with age and mottled with greenish-black mold. She eyed the black, muddy floor, cracked and strewn with rubble. The walls were grimy and splattered with deep stains, like an old dungeon. It smelled of mold and decay, and small rodent eyes stared out from holes in the walls.

"Can you climb down, Corey?" Leila called upward as she reached the bottom.

Corey was shaking. "Are you serious? I have four legs!"

Philbert held Corey around his chest and lowered him into the pit. Corey's rear legs dangled just above Leila's upstretched hands, so she climbed up two rungs. "Don't be afraid, Corey," she urged.

"Honestly, I feel like an idiot," Corey replied.

Leila felt Bee's hands steadying her from below as she grabbed Corey. She set him carefully on the floor, and Philbert scampered down the ladder after her. He skipped the last two steps and landed with a thud.

"Is this your headquarters?" Leila asked.

"Almost there," Bee said. "No one likes to use this entrance, but it was the closest. Easiest location for street parking. Let's do this."

Philbert inserted a key into a hole and pushed on the wall. With a deep, echoing groan, a door swung open.

Immediately Corey's knees buckled and he began to howl. "Sto-o-o-op that!"

"Stop what?" Leila asked.

"Oh dear." Philbert stepped through the door and

tapped out a code on a wall panel. "Sorry about the sound. Humans can't hear it, but animals can. It's to dissuade unwanted visitors. It also sets off visual alerts so we can detect if the infiltrator is human. We have additional alarms beyond this. Security is our middle name. Now let's step into the entry chamber for detox. We try to keep the place as sterile as possible."

Leila followed him through the door into a harshly lit underground room. The walls were made of bright blue tiles, the floor shiny gray marble. Long benches lined one of the walls. Two of the others were mounted with white shelves containing clear, size-labeled Lucite boxes—shoes, white uniforms, masks, caps. A couple of shower stalls stood at the opposite end of the room, their glass doors ajar.

"We'll quickly shower, change, and then move into the main headquarters," Philbert said, a smile growing across his face. "They cannot wait to meet a real live Throwback."

"I'll shower and dress, and then I'll wash Corey," Leila volunteered.

"*What?*" Corey looked at her in horror. "You will not!"

"What are you embarrassed about?" Leila said. "Hate

to break it to you, but you have not been wearing pants this whole time."

Corey growled. "Some friend."

A winding tunnel led deeper into the complex under Central Park. Corey's paws clicked sharply on the cement floor. The walls were rounded and polished, reflecting Leila, Bee, Philbert, and Corey as they walked. Strips of multicolored light overhead gave the whole thing a cheery Christmas-in-outer-space effect.

Bee, Leila, and Philbert wore crisp white coveralls emblazoned with an orange K, for Knickerbockers. After his shower, Corey's fur looked fluffy and clean.

"This is crazy," Leila said, looking around in awe. "I mean, thousands of people are jogging right above us. They have no idea what's under them. There's plumbing, oxygen . . . how was this place built without anyone seeing it?"

"It was built in full sight," Bee replied. "In 1859, by a Knickerbocker named Frederick Law Olmsted. It's been renovated since then."

"Wait. As in, the guy who designed this park?" Leila blurted. "*That* Olmsted? Built *this*?"

"Smart girl," Philbert remarked.

"He also designed Prospect Park, Fairmont Park in

Philadelphia, the Capitol grounds in Washington. He based the designs on the great parks of Europe."

"Show-offs," Corey muttered.

"In the 1800s New York was growing like crazy," Bee said. "It had become industrial, sooty, crowded, smelly. There were no public parks here. This area here was farmland, swamps, small villages, rocky outcroppings. Around 1810 the city divided the area up into a street grid. But as the population grew and trains were built, people began floating the idea of a great park. The government held a competition and Olmsted won."

"They didn't know they'd hired a time traveler— haw!" Philbert continued. "Olmsted was obsessed with the past because he spent lots of time there!"

"Wait, people knew about time travel back then?" Leila asked.

Philbert nodded. "The federal government was secretly studying it. They never allocated quite enough money, even though the young secretary of the navy was a time traveler, too. Then the president declared time travel a hoax. He ordered the money stopped and the files destroyed. So one night those files were smuggled out of the White House by that very same navy secretary. You see, he had once been police commissioner of New York City. He and Olmsted were—how you do say it?—BFFs. His name was Theodore Roosevelt."

"Shut up!" Leila said.

"As you wish," Philbert replied.

"That's an expression," Bee explained. "It means keep talking."

"I see," Philbert said, looking confused. "Olmsted and Roosevelt took the group private. They also kept it secret and gave it the name Knickerbockers. Word spread by way of secret handshakes, pins, coded newspaper ads. Members took an oath of confidentiality. But it proved difficult to hold meetings. When Olmsted got the commission to build Central Park, it was a dream come true. He had access to diggers, blasters, and tunneling equipment."

"So he built this—underground—while he was building Central Park?" Leila asked.

Philbert nodded. "This park looks natural, but every inch was planned. They cut down trees, dug tunnels for water pipes and electricity, moved boulders, dynamited bedrock, built roads. They created lakes, waterfalls, and scenic views out of swamps. They sculpted rubble and soil into hills and overpasses. A reservoir was built to supply drinking water. The public was not allowed in during construction. Olmsted swore workers to secrecy. No one knew this headquarters was being built. It just looked like part of the excavation."

"They hired specialists to help design it," Bee added. Years later, the great escape artist Houdini helped design a new security system. He was a Knickerbocker, too. You'd be amazed at how many famous people were."

Now she was pushing open a door to a circular balcony above a large windowless office, with beige walls and fluorescent lights overhead. Ten or so people worked in cubicles, wearing earbuds and intently staring at screens. "Welcome to our hall of heroes," Philbert said.

The walls of the curved balcony were festooned with framed portraits. "Einstein . . . " Leila said. "Theodore Roosevelt . . . Harriet Tubman . . ."

"Annie Oakley the Wild West sharpshooter," Bee continued, pointing as she identified the images, "Frederick Douglass, Ben Franklin, Jules Verne, Marie Curie, Ernest Shackleton, Frida Kahlo. Those are the definite time travelers, ones who actually wrote about it. Most of their accounts are under lock and key. There's also evidence for Plato, Lao-tzu, Virginia

Woolf, Beethoven, Queen Elizabeth I, Shaka Zulu, even Buddha."

"Wow . . ." Leila said.

Under the portraits were glassed-in display cases. Each case contained crazy artifacts—like a handwritten report by Ben Franklin titled "Being a First-Hand Report on the Traversal of Time," and a drawing of a bearded guy in old-timey clothes facing a dinosaur and signed *Jules Verne*. But the one that really drew Leila's eye was a polished wooden box with a brass plaque:

TO THE IMMEASURABLE MEASURE OF TIME: DEDICATED TO A LOST KNICKERBOCKER

BY FREDERICK LAW OLMSTED. MARCH 21, 1861.

"Who's the lost Knickerbocker?" Leila asked.

Bee shrugged. "Some time-traveling friend maybe?"

Leila lifted the glass door and opened the box. She extracted a battered old pocket watch frozen at 3:15, with a note that read, "19th-c pocket watch, found 2011 during SV excavation."

"SV would be Seneca Village," Philbert said. "A community that was evicted in order to build Central

Park. There were several settlements in the park's area, but Seneca Village was perhaps the largest and most established. The residents were mostly working- and middle-class African Americans, and they were paid by the city to settle elsewhere. The park was being built in 1861, and we figure Olmsted either buried this or misplaced it. It was found during a twenty-first-century excavation."

Leila put the watch on the shelf next to its box. She looked up at a bank of monitors near the ceiling. They showed a couple of dozen views—a subway platform, bunker-like rooms, a hospital operating room, and five locked doors.

"There are quite a few entrances to our headquarters throughout the park. One is directly out of the subway tunnel along Fifty-Ninth Street. Another in the men's room of the Conservatory Garden. A little hut on Central Park West and a hundred and fourth, a small electrical substation in the Ramble. Behind a waterfall in the North Woods—"

"The place where I first met Smig," Corey remarked.

"Smigzactly." Philbert looked over the room, clapped his hands loudly, and raised his voice. "People! Look up, please! I am proud to announce the arrival of our honored guest and first-ever Throwback, Master Corey Fletcher!"

"Wait," Leila said. "When are you going to tell us your genius plan?"

Philbert and Bee ignored her question. Their eyes were focused on the workers below. The curious ones looked up from their screens. They did double-takes at Corey. They elbowed each other.

And then, one by one, they all shoved their chairs back and stood, applauding.

A whoop rang out from behind them in the hallway. In minutes the place was jam-packed with people smiling, laughing, and whispering Corey's name.

Bee beamed at Corey. "You're a star! How does it feel?"

"What am I supposed to do, wave?" Corey said.

"This is freaking me out," Leila murmured to Bee. "How many people work here? I thought you said we were going to help Corey, not put him on display!"

"Everyone back to work, please!" Philbert called out. As people drifted away, he turned toward Leila. "Helping Corey is precisely what we intend to do. Ipso facto, we require the talents of a Throwback, in order to reverse the events that led to his transspeciation—"

"No," Corey snapped. "And also, no."

"Corey—" Bee pleaded.

"I told you before," Corey said. "I screw up every-thing. No matter what I try to do, the opposite happens. I'll just end up nuking the world."

Philbert sighed. "Hear me out—"

"What part of 'no' don't you understand?" Corey growled. He was baring his teeth now. "This is all they've got? Sending me into the past again? Pressuring us in front of all these people? They tricked us, Leila."

Leila knelt, wrapping her arm around his neck. "This isn't like you, Corey," she said.

"Well, I'll get out of everyone's way then. Bye."

Corey shook loose from Leila's grip and sprang toward the door. With a flurry of screams and gasps, the lingering Knickerbocker workers leaped back, col-liding into each other in the hallway.

"Corey, no!" Leila shouted.

"We don't want to send you back to change the past!" Bee added. "That's not our plan!"

Corey stopped in the doorway and turned. "You said you needed a Throwback. I am the only Throw-back here, right?"

Philbert cast a nervous glance toward Bee. "You wanted to know about our secret project, yes?" he asked. "Well, erm, the plan involves a team of top geneticists and microsurgeons. You see, we intend to create a Throwback."

"Wait," Leila said. "*Create* one? Like Frankenstein? Cutting someone open and putting in the Throwback parts?"

"In not quite so brutal a manner," Philbert said. "This is the twenty-first century. The procedure will be refined and painless."

"The point is to save Corey's life," Bee added. "By . . . well, cloning his talents, so to speak."

Philbert stepped toward Leila. "All we need," he said, "is the right volunteer."

13

This time Corey jumped at Philbert.

As the old guy screamed, leaping back into the hallway, Leila lunged for Corey. She dug her fingers into his back, grabbing a hunk of fur and skin. "Stop this right now! What has gotten into you?"

Corey glared at Philbert. "The answer is no. I don't want to mess up the past—and I don't want you to, either!"

"Let's just hear them out!" Leila insisted.

"And let them turn you into some science experiment?" Corey replied. "What if it doesn't work? What if you die?"

"Corey . . ." Leila knelt by him and stroked his fur, whispering in his ear. "No one's forcing us. *We* make the rules. I say we listen to them and ask questions. I agree to let you make the final decision."

Corey grumbled. "My final decision will be no. I don't want any more of this, Leila. Because if anyone can make things worse, it's me. And I don't want to see what 'worse' is!"

"I don't believe you, Corey. I think you want your life back. I want you to have your life back."

"Why?" Corey growled. "What's it to you?"

"Because . . ." Leila felt her voice bottling up in her throat. She missed Corey. Missed him so much. "Because I just do."

"Dude, I think she likes you," Bee murmured.

Leila closed her eyes and turned away. "Did you have to say it like that?"

"If there's the tiniest possibility of hope, Corey, don't you want to hear it?" Bee continued. "Okay, if you two discuss this and say no, we'll respect that. Deal?"

Corey didn't turn back. But Leila thought she could see the tiniest hint of a nod.

"Go on, tell us your plan," she said softly.

The other workers had backed down the hallway, and the room was empty. Philbert eyed Corey cautiously. "If there's one thing we have here," he said, "it's a team of cutting-edge geneticists. Around ten years ago they isolated the sequence in the genome that indicates the ability to hop in time."

"Meaning they could examine a drop of anyone's blood and know whether they're a time traveler," Bee said. "Now they believe they've found the exact location for the Throwback ability on the gene map."

"Every time traveler has an identical gene sequence for time-hopping ability," Philbert continued. "Except for one spot. One place on the gene map. We call it Section 13819a, and it varies crazily from one person to the other."

"If the Section 13819a genes have a certain pattern— boom, you have the Tracker ability, like you and I do," Bee said.

"Me?" Leila replied. "How do you know—?"

"More about that later," Bee said. "The point is, we're pretty certain the Throwback gene pattern would also appear in Section 13819a."

"So . . . if they examine Corey's Section Whatever," Leila said, "they'll record his sequence. And then they'll know exactly what makes a Throwback."

"Yes," Bee replied.

"And how do I fit in?" Leila asked.

"A Tracker has certain heightened powers," Bee

said. "We think Trackers are much better candidates to become Throwbacks."

"You've heard of gene editing, yes?" Philbert continued. "A little snip-snip here, snip-snip there. In theory, you may be able to remove the part of the gene that gives you, say, diabetes. And then, zzzzip, in goes a healthy piece. Patient cured!"

Corey snorted. "So you want to snip out my Throwback ability?"

"More like a copy-paste," Bee said. "Our scientists would copy the Throwback part of the gene and map it onto . . . well, someone else."

Leila couldn't believe her ears. "Wait. So you'd be able to turn *any* time traveler into a Throwback? Anyone could go back and change the past? Like, everyone here? That's insanely dangerous!"

"I would die before saying yes to that," Corey growled.

"We wouldn't take this lightly," Philbert protested. "But look, we've waited generations for the appearance of a Throwback. And now—voilà!—here is the first one! The Adam of Throwbacks! Let me make our real motive clear. We want to harness and control Throwback ability. As guardians of time travel, we want to prevent damage, not cause it."

"We know you don't want to time travel again, Corey," Bee said. "We understand the trauma you've been through. But you don't have to give up your chance at being Corey again. Thirteen-year-old-boy Corey. With his family. Let someone else be a Throwback. Let *Leila* save you."

"Best-case scenario, Corey, you become human and we gain invaluable insights into time travel," Philbert said. "And in due time, when all has returned to normal, we . . . rearrange your genes and Leila's. Easy peasy. You become normal time travelers. Like your grandfather. Without the ability to change history. You benefit the world by preventing these mistakes from ever happening again. It is the only ethical choice."

Leila's eyes focused on Corey. Animals were supposed to be incapable of facial expression. And maybe he wasn't showing anything at all. Maybe she was just reading his mind, because she knew him as if he were a brother. But she saw every emotion he was feeling right now.

Confusion. Anger. Distrust. Despair.

But there was a flicker in his eye, a glint of hope like a budding flower in a pile of rubble. She couldn't bear to see that die out.

"Okay, thanks," she said to Philbert. "Now let Corey and me talk about this. Privately."

But Corey was staring at her. "Leila, what do *you* want to do?"

Philbert and Bee, who were heading out the door, stopped. Leila felt Corey's eyes burning into her. He wanted an answer now.

She thought hard. She missed Corey so much. She would give anything to see him bouncing up the block toward her house before school, his big mop of hair flopping in the breeze, his shoes untied. "I want you to be you again. If me being a Throwback means I have a chance to save you, then, yeah. I want to do it."

Corey didn't reply for a long time. Then he turned his head and vomited.

"Oh dear," Philbert exclaimed.

"*Corey?*" Leila said.

"I'm not feeling well," Corey replied. "If . . . if . . . you want to do this . . . procedure, I won't stop you."

Leila didn't trust herself to speak. If she thought about it for more than a second, the idea seemed absolutely crazy. She had no guarantee it would work or that she wouldn't be hurt. She had a better head on her shoulders than to agree to something like that.

But sometimes it wasn't about the head.

She met Philbert's steady gaze, and then Bee's. "Let's get started before I change my mind."

Mom

I spoke to rachel's mom & she said u were not there last night . . .

Rachel? Did I say rachel? I am sooooo sorry. Im at randis house. In bed-stuy. She's new in class and I didn't want to say no when she invited me. So much homework & it got late & I didn't want to text u . . .

U exasperate me

Leila put her phone away. Lying to her mom made her feel nauseated. Someday she would be able to explain what was happening. But for now, she had to stick around here and follow the plan.

After the previous night's "pre-op," she'd shared a bunk-bed room with Bee, who snored all night long. So now, sitting next to Bee at breakfast, Leila had no appetite.

The Knickerbockers dining area felt like a miniature version of the Frederick Ruggles Middle School cafeteria, only with older people. They were all still unbelievably excited to see Corey. He was sitting on a comfy gold-colored dog cushion, next to an enormous bowl full of brown lumpy mush. Every time he paused to answer a question, people squealed with delight.

"His mood has improved a little since yesterday," said Bee.

Leila set her scrambled eggs aside. Even looking at them made her stomach feel worse. "I'm scared."

Bee moved her chair closer and took Leila's hand. "Hey, first of all, the procedure will not hurt. You'll have time to recuperate while they evaluate the results, Leila."

"How long will I have to be here?" Leila asked.

"Maybe a week or two," Bee said. "Maybe a couple

of months, max? It's experimental. They may have to redo it. You have to be patient. You've come this far—"

"But I'm a kid, Bee! What am I supposed to tell my mom? I'm already lying to her!"

Bee shrugged. "Look, if this procedure works—I mean *when* it works—history will be rewritten anyway. Corey will be Corey again, right? Which means you never had the need to leave home with a wolf. Your mom's memory will adjust. The only people who will know what happened are Trackers and Throwbacks. Meaning you, Corey, and me."

"What is so special about being a Tracker?" Leila demanded. "Why won't you tell me?"

Bee took a deep breath and leaned forward. "Okay, you *remember* the old Corey, right? I mean, before he transspeciated? You recalled everything about Corey's past, even though no one else did. When you mentioned him to Smig and Auntie Flora, they didn't know who he was."

Leila nodded. "Right. Their memories had adjusted. Mine hadn't."

"Exactly," Bee said. "You have the ability to see multiple pasts. I see them, too. *That's* what a Tracker does. We track the progress of time. When the past is changed, we can see the *before* and the *after*. It's a unique ability."

Leila put down her fork and rubbed her eyes. "Tell me if I have this right: I live a whole life. I have a friend named Corey. I have memories of him and all these things we did together. So that's my reality. Then something happens, and it's all gone. Right?"

"Right."

"Okay. And now there's a new reality. Corey was never born. Yet—abracadabra!—he still exists, as a wolf. Even though he shouldn't. And I still remember him as a kid. Even though he was never a kid. Right?"

"Right again."

"But there is only one reality! So how can I see two?"

"Because both realities exist. Because time doesn't travel in a line, the way we were taught. It's more like a subway map. The trains start on one track, but there's a switching point. The tracks split. Some trains break away and then loop back in. Others go to the Bronx, Manhattan, Queens, Brooklyn. Then they branch into neighborhoods. More switching points. Time is like that, too. Think of how many things happen because of a slight mistake, a fraction of an inch, something unseen or barely heard. A person hears a bird, looks up, and is hit by a car. If she doesn't hear the bird, she lives. If the driver notices her instead of checking the GPS, if the bird chirps just a little softer so she doesn't hear it, she lives. Sometimes time will slip. In one path, the person lives, in the other, no. Different realities branch off, unseen by the others forever."

"It's what Corey's Papou said," Leila murmured. "He explained this all to us."

Bee nodded. "To him, it is a theory. Only a Tracker can confirm it's real."

"So if a Tracker can see all of these realities, how come I never have?" Leila asked.

"You see the paths you're involved in," Bee said. "In my life, there have been near-tragedies. My brother got pulled out by an undertow at the beach. He was rescued, but just barely—in this reality. But sometimes, especially in my dreams, I connect with something dark and deep, a world where he did not survive. The mind tries to block it out, but it's there. Because time split. And on one branch, he did not survive."

Leila nodded, thinking back to nights in her bedroom. "So many dreams . . ." she murmured. "I wake up screaming. Nightmares. Something happened to mom. Or my friend Rachel. My shrink has all kinds of explanations. . . ."

"Your shrink is doing the best he or she can," Bee

replied. "Now, let's talk about Throwbacks. A Throwback is a human being with the power to *create* these switching points in time. A Throwback can make what we call a chaos loop, a branch of time that bubbles out and back in again. Corey made several of them. Including this one."

Bee grabbed a napkin and began to draw:

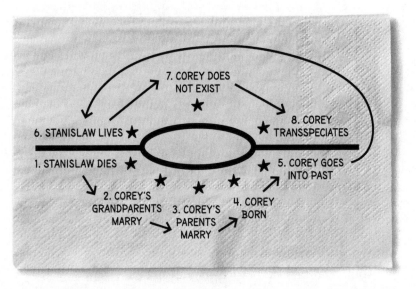

"I'm a terrible artist," Bee said.

Leila stared at the drawing closely. "So . . . the reality that every normal person knows is the latest one—six, seven, and eight. Top of the loop. The bottom is canceled out."

"Yes, it is canceled in the brains of so-called normal

people." Bee smiled. "But you and I, Leila, we see both sides. That is our skill. It's in our genes."

Leila stared at the drawing for a good minute. It made sense. In an insane sort of way. "And if this procedure works, and I become a Throwback," Leila said, "afterward I can go back to Germany. I can unloop the loop that Corey made."

Bee nodded. "But we'd be foolish to send you to a frozen forest in a war zone right away. It's too risky. We'll send you on one or two preliminary controlled time hops first. To test if you really do have the power. We're waiting for the okay on those tests from our national committee."

"You have a national committee?"

"It's very political. They argue over the dumbest things." Bee's phone dinged, and she looked down. "Sorry, it's Dr. Yates. She's in charge of the procedure. Let me get to a quieter place."

As Bee walked away, talking into the phone, Leila glanced at Corey. He was on his side now, still and lifeless. She couldn't see any motion in his chest. "Corey?" she called out, standing up from her seat. "*Corey!*"

She ran to him. As she knelt, shaking his body, the cafeteria fell silent.

Corey's eyes flickered open. "No more dog food,"

he growled. "I hate dog food."

"Leila!" Bee called out from behind her. "What happened? Is he okay?"

Leila stood. "He's sick, Bee. I don't think we can wait for preliminary—"

"I have some amazing news," Bee declared. "They worked all night. They've mapped out the gene sequence. It's a breakthrough. They are so ready for you. You name the time."

Corey was settling back into a sleep. He hadn't touched his food.

Leila took a deep breath. "How about now?"

15

"Count backward from twenty and you'll be asleep, dear," said the nurse through a mask.

Yeah, right.

Leila was the worst sleeper ever. She lay there for a moment on the operating bed. The sleep medication wasn't working, of course. When she felt a tap on her shoulder, she said, "Give it a minute. It takes me forever to—"

"You're done, honey."

Leila glanced up to see an older woman wearing scrubs. Her eyes smiled at Leila through gold-rimmed glasses.

"*What?*" Leila said.

"I'm Dr. Yates," the woman replied. "The propofol put you right out. You've been asleep for half an hour."

"That's impossible!" Leila sat up. A roomful of smiles surrounded her. Bee and Philbert were among them, also dressed in scrubs, along with some medical people and researchers she'd only just met. "That's it? That's the procedure? I'm done?"

Corey was sitting in the corner, looking about as lively as a sack of potatoes. "Sup?" he asked. "How do you feel?"

Leila took a deep breath, looked around, and stretched. "The same. That's bad, right? I don't feel different at all. What's it supposed to feel like when you become a Throwback?"

"How should I know?" Corey replied. "I was born that way."

Taking off her mask, Dr. Yates sat next to Leila. "We were able to analyze Corey's genetic sequence. We think we got it. We also think the editing went perfectly. And, best of all, the sequence appears to be mapped onto your genome."

"Wow," Leila said. "So now we need to test if it worked, right? To see if I'm really a Throwback?"

"Correct," Dr. Yates replied with a nod. "We're

waiting for the committee to come up with a list of micro-hops into the recent past—"

"Micro-hops?" Leila said. "No. Just no—"

"To alter history in an ethically responsible way. Meaning, no harmful consequences. We'll pick one. Being a Tracker, Bee will be able to tell us if you succeeded in changing history. If it fails, we will give it another chance, and then another, and so on."

A sudden choking noise from Corey made them all turn. He coughed up some blood-speckled goop, then let out a hissing fart that filled the room.

As he settled back down, Corey let out a hissing fart that filled the room. Bee turned a shade of green and started backing into the hallway. "It wasn't me," Corey muttered.

It should have been funny, but it wasn't. Dr. Yates lifted an eyebrow and began feeling Corey's abdominal area, then scribbled something on a clipboard. "Gotta go," she said, quickly cleaning up his mess with a wad of towels. "As soon as you feel okay, Leila, you can go back to your room. I'll be in touch later."

The fart was the least of Leila's worries. As soon as she was alone with Corey, she slid off her bed and knelt by him. "What's up with you?"

"I'm fine." Corey's eyes moved toward her. "You?"

"You're not fine. You're sick. Did you hear what she said? I have to wait for some committee. I can't do that. I need to get you back to normal!"

"It would be really dumb to just go back to Nazi Germany alone, Leila," Corey said. "What if the operation didn't work? You could die. They're right. You should do a test first. Scientifically."

"I'll do one of my own!" Leila replied. "Like, now. How hard could it be? Hop into the recent past, change something minor, and see if it sticks. Something that doesn't mess up history."

"Famous last words," Corey said.

"I'll need a relic." Leila began pacing. "What about that old historical stuff—on the balcony that overlooks that room? I'll find something that has metal. It'll take me back to the time when the relic first existed. And I'll . . . bury it or something. When I come back to the present, I'll see if the relic is still in the cabinet. Easy peasy."

"Please don't say that," Corey drawled. "Okay, here's the problem—duplication."

"Huh?"

"When we were in Nazi Germany, I came back to

the present. I met myself. Two Coreys existed at the same time. When I brought my great-uncle Stanislaw's cigarette case into the past, he still had his. It was duplicated. So if you bring a relic back, two of that relic will exist."

"So?"

"So whoever left it could still leave it. You'd just be hiding the duplicate."

"Then I'll nuke them both," Leila said.

Before Corey could protest, she scooted out of the room. The hallway was empty. The only sounds were the soft buzz of air-conditioning ducts and the distant clatter of fingers on keyboards.

Leila kept walking, peering into doors until she found the hall of heroes. She ducked inside, onto the circular balcony. Below her in the control room, people worked intently at their desktops. No one looked up as she tiptoed along the bank of glassed-in cabinets. In the fluorescent lights, something inside one cabinet glinted at her.

Frederick Law Olmsted's watch. She had never put it away after taking it from its box.

She moved closer. The watch sat on a shelf, its glass face shiny but its brass casing dull and tarnished. Leila once again read the inscription on the wooden box:

TO THE IMMEASURABLE MEASURE OF TIME: DEDICATED TO A LOST KNICKERBOCKER

BY FREDERICK LAW OLMSTED. MARCH 21, 1861.

Leila quietly opened the cabinet's glass door and took out the watch. She held it close and turned it over, running her fingers over an engraving of Olmsted's initials on the back, FLO.

She didn't know why Olmsted would have dedicated the watch to a missing friend and then buried it in a box. But if Olmsted had anything, it was vision. He was a guy who looked at swamps and saw lakes. He knew about time travel. Maybe he knew that burying it would preserve it until the future. Maybe he expected someone to bring it back to him.

Maybe this was exactly what Leila was meant to do.

She would show it to Olmsted. She would make him agree not to leave the original watch in the box. Boom. When she came back to the present, she would check. If there was no watch, she was a Throwback. No one would be harmed.

Easy peasy.

Leila felt the brass growing warm in her hand. She knew what that meant.

It always scared her to travel into time. It did weird things to her body and mind. But sometimes, a girl had to do what a girl had to do.

She held tight and closed her eyes.

A girl had to do what a girl had to do. . . . A girl had to do what a girl had to do. . . .

She repeated it over and over in her brain, until the world blasted into solid white.

This time when she awoke, it was because of a scream.

Leila forced her aching eyelids open. Her elbows, ankles, and knees hurt, as if her body had been pulled apart like taffy and then pasted together again.

As she sat up, a frazzled-looking girl stared out from behind a pile of rocks. She looked a couple of years older than Leila, and she wore a long dress buttoned to her neck. "Dear Lord . . ." she murmured, grabbing on to a boulder for stability, "I must give up that sacramental wine."

"Sorry," Leila said. "I didn't mean to scare you."

"Nothing was there," the girl said. "And then . . . you were."

Leila stood, her eyes focusing on a big old construction site around her. In the distance, behind giant piles of rubble and a few rickety cranes, was a line of elegant-looking brownstones. "Is this Central Park?" she asked. "And that street is Central Park West?"

"That is Eighth Avenue," said a deep male voice. "And, yes, this is to be Central Park. Or so they tell us."

An older man stepped out from behind one of the piles. He wore a brimmed hat and clerical collar, and his smile revealed uneven teeth. "Good morning to you, lass."

"Why is she dressed like that, Father?" the girl whispered. "In trousers, like a man?"

"Ask her, Sarah," the man suggested. "I don't imagine she will bite you."

As Sarah tried to put together a question, another voice boomed out, "Ho there! What on earth are you doing here, Reverend Hollingsworth?"

Leila turned to see a thin man in a striped wool coat walking briskly toward them with a pigeon-toed gait. He wore a cap, pulled tightly over dark, dust-caked hair that bounced like earflaps. His visor cast a shadow over slatted, unfriendly eyes and a drooping walrus mustache.

"Good morning, Commissioner Olmsted," Reverend Hollingsworth said, removing his hat. "A little warm for this time of year."

"Wait, *Olmsted?*" Leila blurted. "As in *the* Frederick Law Olmsted?"

"Yes yes," the man said impatiently.

Leila couldn't believe her luck. "You're—you're the guy I came to see!"

As he approached, Leila held out the watch. But Olmsted's angry eyes were focused on Reverend Hollingsworth. "I must insist you continue your conversation beyond the confines of the park, as the workday has commenced. I confess I am surprised with you, Reverend. You know this area is closed."

"Sir," Leila said, "I'm with the Knick—"

"I apologize, Commissioner," Reverend Hollingsworth cut in, his words spilling out in a torrent, "but my petitions to your office have gone unanswered. My daughter and I are searching for valuables lost when our home was destroyed. We were unable to move until receiving payments from the city, which as you know were delayed by the bond crisis. My parishioners report that some possessions were found by the kind gentlemen who work for you. So I thought—"

"Good grief, this is no longer Seneca Village, dear man," Olmsted snapped. "This is a construction site for a park! We are leveling this area with explosives drilled into solid granite. These are detonated daily, often from remote locations where workers cannot see trespassers. Hence the warning signs on Eighth Avenue. It is sheer insanity to be here right now! I shall leave, and you will follow. Come!"

"*Sarah!*" the reverend yelled, running around the rock pile. "*Sarah, where are you?*"

"Mr. Olmsted, just a second!" Leila said. "Don't go. I need to talk to you!"

Leila heard other voices, shouting. She looked up to see three men in overalls, gesturing at her from a distance, screaming, waving their hats toward the park exit.

Olmsted was already heading toward the street. "We shall talk on the sidewalk!" he commanded. "Come now, foolish child, before I summon the constables!"

Closing her fist over the watch, Leila began to sprint after Olmsted. She veered around the giant outcropping.

As she prepared to run, it exploded before her eyes.

Her body lurched upward into the air, and her feet left the ground in a spew of debris.

16

Leila hit the ground hard, landing on her hands and forehead.

Her heart beat furiously as she caught her breath. She tried to push herself upward but dust settled around her like a smothering fist. Through the cloud's thickness she heard muffled shouts but saw no one. Grit rushed into her nose and mouth, and she coughed until her throat felt like sandpaper.

Her hands were empty. The watch was gone.

Had she slipped it into her pockets? She dug her hands inside, but they were empty. Everything had fallen out. Not only the watch, but her phone and her coins.

Which meant she had no way to get back.

With one palm over her mouth, she crawled around the area, desperately feeling the ground. But her eyes stung, and soon her breaths came in deep, racking heaves. She would have to come back later.

The dust was thicker to her right, so she stood and ran to her left. Hacking and spitting, she reached a solid rock wall about ten feet high. Looking to each side into the dust clouds, she couldn't tell how long it was. But to the right was a set of stairs, leading to a tiny building perched at the top of the wall.

Taking the stairs two at a time, she screamed "*Hello?*" through her coughs. At the top she pulled on the door handle, but the place was locked tight.

Below her, over the other side of the wall, stretched an expanse of water. A rectangular reservoir divided by a stone walking path. It wasn't at all like the Central Park reservoir she knew, which was bigger and shaped like a giant amoeba. But it was the only place free of dust.

She thought about jumping in. The water would be cool. The air would be free of dust.

But she wasn't that boneheaded.

Near the hut, a ladder led down the inner wall toward the water. Three or four steps down would be enough. Her face would be shielded. She could peek back over when it all cleared.

She ran toward it, spitting dust, coughing. Slowly she lowered herself over the edge. The rungs were slippery. Her body shook with coughing.

"Hey!" a voice cried out.

Leila looked up toward it.

And she fell in.

The water was frigid. It jolted her body. She quickly broke the surface, letting out a loud gasp. Treading to keep afloat, she noticed a steep rock cliff looming over the water. She knew where this was. In the present day, a miniature castle called Belvedere stood on that cliff. This reservoir, in modern times, had become an oval-shaped field dotted with baseball diamonds called the Great Lawn.

But the last thing she needed was to die of exposure and be buried under it.

Shivering, she swam back toward the wall. A man with a lantern appeared at the top. He wore a white cloth mask over his mouth and carried a round life preserver, which he threw out to Leila.

She grabbed on to it, kicking her legs toward the ladder. Gripping the rungs, she climbed. At the top, he handed her a mask like his, then took off his jacket and wrapped it around her. It was thick and warm.

"Th-thank you," Leila said. "I d-d-didn't mean to jump. Just wanted to g-g-get away from the d-d-dust."

"I get it—yeah, usually them explosions ain't big like this!" the guy said with a thick New York accent. He wore a cap like Olmsted's, but he looked older and was built like a bear. "Looks like the end of the world, don't it? They says they're making a park for the people? Ha! Plenty of people used to live here—houses, farms, churches, goats. Now it's just rats and hawks. It's a wonder you didn't get killed by the dynamite! Can I help you home?"

"No, thanks." Leila glanced around, feeling dazed. The dust was settling now and patches of sky peeked through the gray blackness. She began heading down the stairs. "But I—I lost this pocket watch. And some money and . . . valuables. Somewhere down there. I really need them. So if you could help me find them, Mr. . . ."

"Clarence Bowers, at your service!" the man said, following her. "I think some of the other guys was hiding from the explosions, behind the big rock. Maybe they can help."

He let out a piercing whistle. At the bottom, he and Leila carefully scoured the area. His lantern wasn't much help. But in a couple of minutes, two other construction workers ran over toward them. After some quick instructions from Clarence, they joined the search.

It took about five minutes before one of them cried out, "Hey, look, it's still tickin'!"

He held out the dust-coated watch, with a triumphant, gap-toothed smile. As Leila reached out, the guy lobbed a glob of spit on it, rubbing it on his grime-covered overalls.

Leila recoiled. "Ew."

"Aw, criminy," Clarence said, snatching the watch from the guy's hand. "Gimme that, Benny. Like animals, these knuckleheads."

"Ayyyy, I was just cleanin' it," the guy named Benny replied.

Clarence scampered back up the stone stairs, disappeared for a moment, and returned with the watch wrapped in a handkerchief. "A bit of pure, clean New York City reservoir water to wash off the dust and gorilla spit," he said.

"Thanks, Clarence." As Leila took the watch, Benny's partner reared back his arm to throw something.

"Fake coins!" he bellowed. "Got crazy dates on 'em —2020, 2018. Bets on if I can make it to the other side of the water?"

Leila's jaw dropped as Benny picked up her cell phone.

"Okay, Sluggo, you t'row that, I'll t'row this thing!" Benny piped up. "Two bits whoever makes it farthest."

Leila dived at them, shrieking. *"Give that to me! All of that is mine!"*

Benny jumped away in shock. He dropped the phone and Leila snatched it out of the dirt.

"Sorry, we was just playing, girly," Sluggo said.

"My name isn't girly!" Leila stood, shaking. "This was supposed to be so easy! In and out. Return a watch, have a chat with Olmsted, go home. Easy bloody peasy! *I don't even know where he is!*"

Her voice died in the thick air as the three men stared, baffled. "Me neither, kid," said Sluggo, thrusting the coins toward her. "You want your money?"

Leila snatched back the coins. She spotted her student ID card on the ground and scooped that up, too.

This whole scheme had been useless. Corey had been right. When you traveled into the past, nothing ever went the way you thought it would. Even something as simple as returning a dumb watch.

She would have to go back and think of a plan B.

But as she held tight to the watch, phone, and coins,

she heard the clopping of hooves draw near.

"Ho, there!" a voice called out. "Have you fellows seen a young woman?"

Clarence stepped forward, chest thrust high. "We ain't all fellas, Constable Bromley. Just 'cause someone wears pants don't mean she's a he."

"Well, right you are!" The constable raised an eyebrow toward Leila, as another man rode up beside him. "I believe we have found our missing girl, Constable Moosup!"

The other constable was bigger than Bromley. He had a compressed face that was locked into a look of confusion. "Hrrm," he said. Shoving two dirty fingers into his mouth, he let out a piercing whistle, then shouted "Found!"

Now footsteps pounded the ground, and through the dust ran Reverend Hollingsworth and his daughter. "Oh, dear girl, you're all right!" the reverend cried out.

But Leila was looking at the figure who was following close behind them. It was Frederick Law Olmsted, in the flesh. His stern expression was now creased with worry.

As she stepped toward them, Leila could feel the watch growing warm in her hand, the coins in the other. Her body was about to time-hop.

No, not yet, she commanded her body.

"Commissioner Olmsted!" she blurted, running toward him. "I'm a Knickerbocker!"

Olmsted's face went rigid. "I beg your pardon?"

"I'm bringing this watch from the future!" She tried to hand the watch to Olmsted, but he jumped back in surprise.

As the watch fell to the dirt, Constable Bromley shouted, "Seize that, Moosup! Is this another stolen item from the good settlers who once lived here?"

"Grrrrr," said Constable Moosup, slowly dismounting his horse.

Olmsted was staring at Leila, but she couldn't read the expression on his face. "Repeat what you said, dear girl?" he asked.

"Why, this appears to be the property of Commissioner Olmsted himself!" Constable Bromley bellowed, reading the inscription on the back of the watch. "Seize that thief!"

Leila felt her student ID card digging into her hand. The coins were red hot. She felt for her pockets, but her hands were shaking. "Mr. *Olmsted,*" Leila said, her words dipping and elongating, as if she were underwater, "*whatever you do, do not put that watch in a wooden box! I need to know if I'm a Throwback!*"

But the plea was lost in a blur of faces that swirled like leaves in the autumn wind. She could hear Olmsted's voice as if from a cavern: "What's that? What did you say?"

Now all Leila could hear were shouts and the panicked whinnying of horses. A dull whoosh grew to a roar, and once again the park exploded around her. This time there was not a speck of dust or a shaking rock, but whirling bright fragments of gray and white.

17

Leila came to consciousness on a soft rubber mat in a warm indoor space. That was the good news.

The bad news was that it smelled like a gym. As she sat up, she groaned. The side of her face ached, her clothes were wet, and her throat still felt gritty. Plus she'd managed to land on a softball, which didn't feel very soft right now.

From the opposite end of the gym, a familiar cheery voice called out, "Hey, don't you have a class to go to, Rip van Winkle?"

It was Ms. Ahmed, the PE teacher. In the gym of Frederick Ruggles Middle School.

None of which made sense. For one thing, the

school was across the street from Central Park, so somehow she'd missed Knickerbocker headquarters by a few blocks.

For another, Ms. Cranmore was her gym teacher this year. Ms. Ahmed had moved to Arizona over the summer. "Um . . . welcome back?" Leila said weakly.

Ms. Ahmed gave her a quizzical glance. And it occurred to Leila that Ms. Ahmed had never left.

Meaning Leila's time hop had gone way wrong. She'd not only missed the return location, but also the correct time period. "Arggh," she murmured. "Does this ever get easy?"

Ms. Ahmed chuckled. "PE is tough, but you'll thank me."

As she went back to her work, Leila turned to go. But she stopped when she heard a burst of laughter from the locker rooms.

"You look like someone stuck you with a cattle prod!" a voice called out.

"I think it's cute," another voice said.

"I'm going to burn mine."

"Mine sucks worse."

Leila recognized all the voices. Including the last one, which was her own.

The wooden risers had been pulled up from the floor and accordioned against the wall, so she hid behind them.

Through the slats she watched the group—herself, Rachel Eisen, Claudia Ramos, and Julie Norman—heading from the locker room to the exit. They were all staring at plastic ID cards, sizing them up. She totally remembered this conversation.

Leila winced at the outfit she'd been wearing that day. It was a plaid skirt she'd bought in a fit of envy over some YouTuber she'd already forgotten. The last time she'd worn that skirt was at the end of the previous school year.

"What the heck . . . ?" she murmured to herself.

Her right hand was cramping up, and she realized she had a death grip on all her stuff she'd recovered after the 1861 blast. Slowly she released her fingers. Along with the coins, her school ID card was there, too. The card's sharp edges had ridged the inside of her palm and fingers.

Her *plastic* ID card. Which had been issued the previous school year. It was on this day, she realized. She remembered this conversation with her friends after gym about how disgusting their ID card photos were.

She looked at her card, baffled. *Metals* got you time

travel, not polymers. Or whatever that stuff was called.

"I thought you just left!" chirped Ms. Ahmed's voice. "I heard you talking with your friends."

Leila spun around. "I did leave! I mean, I did but I came back. Because I forgot . . . um, this!"

As she held out her card, Ms. Ahmed gave her a nod and disappeared into a supply closet.

That was when Leila noticed the small square chip on the card. The one the administration had made such a big deal out of. The ultimate in security. It shone with whatever substance it was made of. Which pretty obviously was metallic.

Leila exhaled. Her palm had made contact with the wrong artifact. The chip was all it took. With a sigh of frustration, she slipped the ID card into her pocket. She willed herself to stay calm. It wouldn't be hard to correct the mistake. This kind of thing had happened to Corey, too—like the time he'd slipped from 2001 to 1917 because of an old photograph that contained silver.

The coins.

Those would get her back. She rummaged in her pockets.

"Leila?" Ms. Ahmed called out. "Is everything okay?"

"Fine!" Leila snapped.

She dumped the coins in her pocket, smiled, and

headed for the door. Right now she needed to find a private place for time-hopping. Away from the eyes of her teacher.

The hallway was full of kids between classes. Most were heading left, in the direction of the front lobby. So Leila headed right.

She walked fast, turning up the collar of Clarence's coat, to cover as much of her face as possible. Kids were flowing in and out of the girls' room, so that wasn't an option. She passed at least five posters for the previous school year's talent show, *Ruggtime!* It hadn't happened yet, but she remembered it well. Claudia had gotten a standing ovation after a dance routine from *Chicago.* Julia had brought the house down with a ballad from *Les Miz.* And Corey, being Corey, had done the craziest thing of all—"improvisational anagrams." Someone would call out a name and Corey would scramble the letters on the spot.

"Edward Diao" became "a weirdo dad." "Theresa Bradley" turned into "leathery breads."

And he had done this *in his head.*

Was Corey even alive? How did Tracker time travel work? Which part of the loop was Leila in—the one where Corey was a human? Or the one where Corey never existed?

146

The Corey loop or the Gregory loop?

She picked up the pace. A left turn at the end of the hallway would lead to a rear exit. It led to a trash area in a side alley. Kids always left through the front.

She took the left quickly, and then she stopped in her tracks. Corey—Human-Corey from the end of last school year—was at the end of the hallway, back to the wall.

That answered her question. She was in the Corey loop.

Ducking back around the corner, she peered carefully around. Corey was preoccupied. His head hung down and his face was red, as if he'd been crying. "It was so stupid to agree to do this," he murmured.

Standing next to him, about five inches shorter, was Papou. The old man's hand rested on Corey's shoulder. "You're going to kill, *paithi mou*, don't worry," he said in his musical, soothing, Greek-accented voice. "It is such an original idea, perfect for talent show. Why? Because it shows real talent! Not just this lip-singing oo-oo-ba-ba-ba-baby making no sense. You do these anagrams in your sleep!"

Corey smiled. "It's lip-*synching*. And you're the one who's the anagram expert, not me."

"No," Papou replied. "I taught you, and now you

run rings around me. Come on. Ready? 'Central Park.'"

Leila stepped back into the other hallway, just out of sight.

"Wait, wait . . . 'prancer talk'!" Corey said.

Papou clapped. "Bravo! How about this one—'smart Corey.'"

"Um . . . 'army escort'?"

"You see? You see, my modest boy? I am so proud of you! You be proud of yourself."

"Thanks, Papou," Corey said.

"S'*agapo, levendi mou*," the old man said softly.

"I love you, too."

Leila recognized the Greek words. The tender way Papou said them always made her wish someone would say them to her.

She snuck a peek around the corner again. Corey was hugging his grandfather now. It looked a little awkward because Corey had grown so much the year before and towered over the old man. But there they were, in profile, with the afternoon sun streaming in from the end of the hallway.

Leila choked back a sob. Right now was only one year ago, but everything was so different. Right now Corey was a human being who didn't yet know he could travel in time. And right now Papou was devoted to him with his heart and soul, not to another kid named Gregory.

It was sweet and painful and something she didn't want to forget. Because in a few minutes, when she hopped away, it would be gone forever.

Quickly she pulled her phone from her pocket and snuck a photo. As she ducked back again, she heard Corey and Papou say good-bye.

A set of footsteps headed her way, and Leila froze.

Corey came bounding around the corner with his long, loping stride. He was staring at the floor, muttering words to himself. Probably anagrams.

She bowed her head, pretending to look in her pockets. But he showed no sign of even looking her way.

Leila didn't realize Corey had a smell. Soap, deodorant, sweat—the moment it reached her nostrils she knew it was him. She would know if you blindfolded her. Being inches away from his . . . *humanness* made her ache. Part of her wanted to run him down, tell him everything that was going to happen, and warn him not to travel into the past, ever.

But she knew that would be truly dumb. As a Throwback, Corey was going to save lives. Leila had to stick to her mission. She needed to return to the present and complete the Olmsted test.

If there was no watch, she was a Throwback. She could unloop the chaos loop Corey had created in Germany. It would preserve just about all the good Corey had done, and also restore him to normal. It would bring him back to his *papou*.

Leila waited until Corey was out of sight. Then she ducked around the hallway again. Papou must have gone out back, because it was empty. He was a fast walker, and he'd be halfway down the block by now.

It was a perfect spot to do what she needed to do.

She stuck her phone in her pocket. She made sure the student ID card was still there, tucked safely out of sight and touch. Taking out her coins only, she stood against the wall and squeezed as hard as she could.

18

When Leila's eyes popped open, she was lying on a bed and Dr. Yates was staring down at her. Exactly the way she'd awakened from the procedure.

For a moment, Leila thought the whole thing had been a dream.

But as she tried to sit, her head felt like it had been smashed with a shovel. "Did I do it?" she demanded. "Did I go back? Because this feels like I never left."

Now Bee was sitting beside her. "Your hair was wet and your face was covered with dust. We helped you wash and change clothes, but you wouldn't wake up for a long time. So, yeah, you did."

"The question is, why?" Dr. Yates asked. "This was not part of the plan."

Leila sat up fully. The doctor was glaring at her.

The watch. She needed to know if it was there.

"Where's Corey?" she asked.

"Excuse me?" Dr. Yates said. "We need to have a discussion."

"Hold that thought," Leila replied. "I'll talk. I promise. After I see Corey! Stay right there."

Before Bee or Dr. Yates could stop her, Leila ran out of the room and down the hall. She barged into Corey's room, but the light was off. "Hey, I'm back," she said.

"Hi, back, I'm Corey," Corey's voice came from the corner. "Did it work? Is the watch gone?"

"I'm about to check the display case," Leila replied. "Want to come?"

"I'll follow. I'm slow."

Leila raced to the control room and pushed open the door. From the doorway she could see the wooden box inside the glassed-in case, exactly where she'd left it. Her heart jackhammered in her chest as she ran closer.

Reaching in, she pulled out the box and opened it.

Corey's footsteps padded weakly on the tiled floor. "Well?" he said.

Leila scooped out a brass pocket watch. She held it to the light. It had the same stains, the same dull brass, the same FLO initials carved into the back.

She felt her body sag. "I'm not a Throwback."

"Well, that sucks," Corey grunted.

Leila stared at it silently, as if the heat from her glare would make the watch disintegrate. Finally, with a strangled cry, she threw it against a wall. It fell to the floor with a thud.

"Didn't break," Corey said with a yawn. "They don't make them like they used to."

"You think this is funny?" Leila snapped. "I nearly died back there. And for what? The genius operation? It was a great big fail, Corey! Don't make me mad, because I'm about to cry."

Corey curled against the wall. "How do you know it was a fail? Something weird could have happened, Leila. Are you sure you did everything exactly right? Tell me what happened, step by step."

"I—I met Olmsted . . . and a preacher," Leila said, "but there was this explosion, and all the stuff fell out of my pockets, and a guy named Clarence had to rescue me from the reservoir, and when I found everything again I got all frustrated and started to come home, but Olmsted came out of the dust with a couple of weird constables just as I was starting to hop, and I told him not to put the watch in the box, and then I touched my

ID card chip and ended up last year in the gym with Ms. Ahmed."

"I . . . I think I got that," Corey said. "So when you told Olmsted not to put the watch in the box, are you sure he heard you?"

Leila thought back. "I was fading away. I shouldn't have been holding on to my metal stuff. Everything was blurry."

"So maybe he didn't hear you." Corey struggled to stand and padded slowly down the circular floor to the open glassed-in cabinet. "That plaque on the box. What does it say?"

"'Dedicated to a lost Knickerbocker,'" Leila replied.

Corey looked up at her with bloodshot eyes. "Maybe that's you. You showed up from the future and disappeared right in front of him, right?"

"That's pretty far-fetched."

"Maybe," Corey said. "All I'm saying is that you don't know. Not yet. Maybe you *are* a Throwback, Leila. The Knickerbockers want to do more tests, right? So don't give up. Do one of theirs."

Leila smiled at Corey. "You're the one telling *me* not to give up? I thought you wanted to remain a wolf."

"I'm about to fart," Corey said.

Leila stepped back. "Not funny."

"Sorry. I can't help it," Corey said. "I feel like my body is aging or something. It sucks to be a wolf."

The stench was unbearable. Leila tried not to let it show as she turned away. "Corey, I have to tell you something. I saw you at school today. Only it wasn't really today. It was almost a year ago. Do you remember the anagram thing you did at the talent show? Remember how nervous you were?"

Corey nodded. "I thought I was going to choke. I thought people were going to make fun of me for the rest of my life."

"You got a standing ovation," Leila reminded him. "You nailed it. Because your *papou* came to school, just to give you a pep talk before rehearsal. You were petrified. But he turned you around like magic. I saw it. It was like he carved a piece out of his own soul and gave it to you."

"That's gross," Corey said. "But yeah."

Leila sighed. "Corey, you have to hang in there. I don't like the way you sound. You're sicker than you think. I'll take another test. And I swear, if it works, I'm heading straight to Germany. I want to get that life back. For both of us."

"Neeee neee neee," Corey said.

"What?" Leila said.

"Those are violins," Corey replied.

"I hate you, Corey Fletcher," Leila said.

"No you don't . . . because I'm . . . too"—Corey was trying to stand again, but his legs wobbled and he fell to the floor—"cute."

Leila raced to Corey and knelt by his side. "What just happened?"

"I'm okay," Corey said. "I—I just need to get back to my room."

He struggled to his feet again. Leila tried to help him up but he shook her off. This time he stepped slowly forward, his legs shaky and tentative.

The smack of the door against the inner wall made Leila spin around. Philbert marched inside, with Bee and Dr. Yates behind him. "What exactly is going on here?" Philbert demanded. "Dr. Yates tells me you ran off in violation of her orders."

Corey bared his teeth and growled.

"Did he attack you, Leila?" Dr. Yates said.

As a trio of masked people in hospital scrubs appeared at the doorway, Leila stood in front of Corey. "He didn't attack me. He collapsed."

"He's been snapping at workers, Leila," Dr. Yates said. "I would advise you to keep your distance. You do not want him to bite you."

"I saw you examining him, Dr. Yates," Leila said. "What's wrong with him?"

"We are awaiting blood tests," Dr. Yates said. "So I can't say for sure. But transspeciation can create serious immune problems. As the body is compromised, the transspeciate may exhibit more aggressive behaviors."

"Sedate him," Philbert said to his workers.

A man holding a syringe moved toward Leila and Corey. Behind him was a man with a kind of lariat and a woman dragging an animal cage.

Corey bared his teeth and growled.

"Don't you touch him!" Leila yelled.

"I'm so sorry, this is for your safety," the man with the syringe said, "and for his."

"Move!" Philbert shouted.

The distraction was all Corey needed. He leaped at the man, his jaw clamping on to his pants.

Philbert screamed. The syringe went flying over the balcony. Someone screamed from below. The man with the lariat fell back into the woman with the cage. Bee backed into the hallway, and Philbert fumbled for his phone.

With a burst of strength Leila didn't expect to see, Corey leaped through the doorway and into the hall. "Leila, follow me!" he growled.

As Corey and Leila ran down the hallway, Philbert was screaming for backup over his phone.

They ducked into Corey's room, and Leila slammed the door shut behind them. "How did you do that?" she said.

Corey groaned, collapsing onto the floor. "Adrenaline."

"We can't stay here, Corey," Leila said. "We have to get out."

"How?" Corey asked. "Ask their permission? We're like prisoners. Lab experiments."

"Let me go," Leila said. "Back to Germany. Now."

"Are you crazy?" Corey said.

"This whole thing could be fixed, Corey! You said I might be a Throwback."

"Right. I said *you might be*. That's not the same as *you are*."

"Do you have any better suggestions?"

Their argument was interrupted by the pounding of footsteps in the hallway. Then the doorknob shook. "Open up!" shouted Philbert's voice. "We need to keep you safe!"

Corey looked toward his closet. "Go," he said.

"Hide in the closet?"

"Get clothes," Corey said. "There are tons of them

in there. Double up. Winter clothes. Coats, sweaters, gloves, hats. The more the better. *Go!*"

"I can't go back to Germany unless I have a relic—"

"Just *go!*"

Leila ran to the closet and pulled it open. It was well stocked with generic Knickerbocker clothing that Corey would never use. She grabbed as much as she could, throwing on two sweaters, a winter jacket, wool pants, thick socks, gloves, a knit hat, and a pair of work boots about three sizes too big. Stepping back into the room, she looked at Corey. "Now what?"

"Where's the cigarette case?" Corey asked.

Before Leila could answer, a fist pounded the door. "Open up!" Bee's voice shouted.

"Stanislaw's case!" Corey repeated softly, his eyes focused on Leila. "You took it. When I came back from the past. I saw you."

Leila reached into the pocket of her pants, which were under the wool pants. As she pulled it out, Corey leaped toward her.

She flinched, pulling her hand away as Corey's jaw closed around the case. "Don't let go," he said through clenched teeth.

"*If you don't open, we will break down this door!*" Philbert bellowed.

Corey's head was tilted upward, the brass case pointed toward her. Only an inch or so protruded from his mouth. "Hurry!" he urged.

The door flew open, smacking against the inner wall. *"Back off—now!"* a voice boomed.

A loud *crrrack* echoed in the room, as Leila's fingers touched the case.

19

By the time she lifted herself from the snow, Leila couldn't feel her ears. She couldn't see much either. She sat up, squinting against a hard, driving snow. She was used to the pain of time travel, but this was something totally different. This kind of cold bit right through your heavy clothing. It numbed every feeling in your body.

"Corey?" she called out, struggling to stand.

Her voice was muffled by the snow-choked air. She blinked against the whiteness as she scanned the area. Overhead, pine branches jerked and swayed like the arms of slow-motion cheerleaders. Leila called his name again but got no answer.

Was he even here?

He had to be. He had held on to the cigarette case. He hadn't let go. But people got separated during time hops. She knew that from experience.

"*Corey!*"

They couldn't have landed far from each other. Leila shook off a layer of snow and began looking for footsteps. She traced out a circle and spiraled out into a wider one. The movement was warming her, head to toe. She was thankful Corey made her take the heavy clothes. He had saved her.

He had learned from his own experience.

But by the third circle she hadn't seen any sign of him. Her voice was growing raw from calling his name in the cold air. Her earlier footsteps were nearly covered up by the falling snow. If she couldn't see them, how was she going to see Corey's?

By the fifth circle she heard a soft drumbeat. It freaked her out, until she realized it was the pounding of her own blood. If Corey had passed out from the stress of time travel . . . if he wandered away in his weakened state looking for her . . . if he was freezing to death somewhere . . .

She didn't want to imagine any of those things. She needed to rest. And to think.

What now?

As the snow started to let up, she leaned against a tree to catch her breath. To examine the area. On the bright side, visibility was getting better by the second. But that didn't help, when all you could see was trees. Hundreds of trees. Corey could have been hidden behind any of them. Or buried under snow.

Leila's eyes welled up. She took a deep breath and told herself he was fine. He was a wolf, and wolves were built for this. Maybe he'd gone off to get food and was on his way back. It might only be a matter of moments until he found her.

As she wiped her cheek, she noticed a brightening ahead of her. Some kind of clearing, maybe. She stepped toward it, cupping her hand to her mouth and calling out for Corey again.

The clearing wasn't very large, and in its center was a gray blot, close to the ground. She picked up her pace. Her boots were way too big, but she managed an awkward trot, lifting her knees high.

The blot turned out to be a small hut, or at least the remains of one. Outside the front sat a lopsided, snow-covered carriage. The hut's front entrance was now a gaping rectangle where a door used to be.

She stepped around the carriage and into the small, darkened room. "Corey, are you here?"

Two mice squealed, scattering into different holes.

Inside, shielded from the wind and snow, she felt warmer. A slanted window on the back wall had long ago lost its glass. Its metal frame had rusted into fragments. Outside it, the sun was starting to peek from behind the clouds. It seemed low in the sky. There wouldn't be much time before darkness. She peered through the hole, hoping Corey might be huddled behind the hut.

No such luck. Time to move on.

As she turned toward the door again, a distant voice stopped her in her tracks. Just one word, in a low and guttural voice.

Pine. Or maybe *fine.* Or *nein.*

Nein was German for *no.* This was a German forest.

Nazi soldiers would be trekking through here, somewhere in the vicinity. They had marched Corey's great-uncle through the woods among a group of prisoners. Leila tried to remember what Corey had said about the incident. The prisoners had been told they were being taken to another camp. But Stanislaw had sensed the Nazis were growing tired and wanted to go back. He'd suspected they would murder the prisoners right there and leave. Somehow he had managed to escape, claiming he needed to go off into the woods to pee. As he hid, he heard the soldiers shoot every last one of the men.

Being found by Nazis was the last thing Leila wanted. She hadn't come this far to die.

She hurried out the door and circled around to the back of the hut. Squatting under the window, she could hear a not-too-distant grunt. A cry of pain. They were close. She hoped they passed the front of the hut, not the back. But neither way would be safe for her. Coiling her legs, she prepared to bolt. Just in case.

No. Stay.

If she ran, they would see her. The trees wouldn't offer much protection. Dressed in dark clothing, she'd be an easy target against the white landscape.

She wished Corey were here. He could be flaky, but he could also be very quick in emergencies. She closed her eyes. *What would Corey do?*

"Keep moving," he answered.

Her eyes sprang open. The voice had been so clear. As if he were really there.

She stood up, peeking over the broken sill of the back window, through the hut. She could see a rectangle of forest through the front door. Two distant figures were moving toward her.

One of them was Corey.

Not Wolf-Corey. The real Corey. Human-Corey of the old loop.

Leila swallowed a gasp. She ducked back under the window. The footsteps were tromping heavily in the snow, closer and closer. In front of her the sun was already setting, casting a pale amber glow on the white landscape.

"It . . . gets dark . . . in the woods . . . early," came the other voice. "Maybe . . . we rest. Ankle . . . hurts."

The voice was deep and halting. An older voice, with an accent that didn't sound quite like German. At least not like the German she and Corey had heard in Munich or Vienna. Stanislaw was Polish, if Leila remembered right. But he also knew German. So an odd accent would make sense.

"The hut doesn't give us any shelter or warmth," Human-Corey said.

Leila nearly leaped up. He was so close.

"We're halfway there," his voice continued. "If there are doctors in Kurtstadt, we should keep going."

"We will not have enough light," Stanislaw said.

In a moment, Leila saw a blink of bright light against the snow to her right. Corey must have had a flashlight or more likely, a phone.

"Aaaagh!" Stanislaw screamed. "*Was ist das?*"

"Make it to Kurtstadt, get healthy," Human-Corey said, "and I'll tell you where to invest your money in a few decades."

It was a cell phone flashlight. And a classic Corey bad joke.

This fit exactly into what Corey had told her. If she remembered the story right, Human-Corey only had a short amount of time before saving his uncle and sealing his own fate.

Staying still was making her cold. She felt herself shivering. Here was the opportunity to do *something*. It was the whole reason they'd come here.

So where was Wolf-Corey when she needed him most?

Leila looked desperately back over her shoulder. He had to be alive. She wanted to jump out and scream *stop!* She wanted to try to change things herself. But only a Throwback could change what Human-Corey was about to do. Normal time travelers couldn't affect the past no matter what they did.

She wished she knew for sure if she was or wasn't a Throwback. She wished there were some kind of clear sign you could see on your body, like a secret mole or an eleventh toe.

But even if she was a Throwback, what *would* she do?

Everything had happened so fast. They hadn't made a plan. They had to keep Corey's grandmother from seeing her brother, Stanislaw, in the hospital—but how could they do that without letting Stanislaw die?

The two were moving away from the hut now, toward the setting sun. Human-Corey was silent, struggling to keep his great-uncle upright. She would have to track them without being seen. At least until she found Wolf-Corey.

The woods were thick. Snow was starting to fall again. If Leila lost track of them, there was a chance Wolf-Corey would find them on his own. They would freak.

Stall them.

Leila stepped out from behind the hut. Her voice felt raw, so she'd have to be loud.

She put both hands to her mouth and breathed deep.

RRRRRAAAWRRRR.

The snort from behind her sounded like the rush of a jet engine. She felt a massive weight slam against her back.

Before she could react, her face hurtled down into the snow.

20

Leila pulled herself upward, spitting and coughing. She scrambled to her feet, turning to face her wolf attacker.

His teeth had closed on her jacket, and now he was chewing on the shredded material. "Well, you're back to your frisky self," she said with a sigh of relief.

Wolf-Corey spat out the shreds and stared at her. Somehow he seemed bigger than he'd been before. In this light, his silvery-gray fur reflected more brownish. "Where have you been?" Leila blurted. "I thought you might be dead!"

Sitting back, Wolf-Corey cocked his head and coughed.

"They just passed us—*you* just passed us, I mean,"

Leila barreled on. "You and Great-Uncle Stanislaw. You're rescuing him. You're on the way to that village. We have to think of something now. We can catch them easily. Any ideas?"

Wolf-Corey's back was arched. As he stood and stepped toward her, he licked his lips.

"Um . . ." Leila said, backing away. "Come on, Corey, concentrate. I can't do this by myself."

Out of the corner of her eye, Leila spotted a motion in the woods. Another wolf. "Oh great," she murmured. "Watch your back."

The other wolf came staggering out from behind a bush. Its head was hung low. It was thin and weak looking.

Leila stiffened as the sun reflected off its silvery coat.

"Uh-oh," it murmured, its eyes fixed on Leila's attacker.

And Leila realized she had misunderstood the last few minutes completely.

"Y-y-you spoke," she squeaked, her eyes darting back to the more-distant brownish attacker. "So . . . the one here close to me . . . is *not* you?"

"*Get away, Leila—now!*" Wolf-Corey shouted from the bushes. "*Just run! I'll find you!*"

Now the first wolf was turning to face Corey, baring its teeth and growling.

"Nice to meet you too, sucker!" Wolf-Corey called out. "Na na na boo boo! *Leila, run! I got this!*"

Leila's legs locked. The brown wolf was leaping over the snow toward Wolf-Corey. It was bigger and healthier looking. Leila looked around for something—anything—she could do to help.

The hut's window was inches away. Its frame was metal, and it was falling apart. She kicked the wall beneath it, once, twice, until the entire frame crashed to the ground in pieces. One of the pieces was a shard about three feet long, its end rusted to a jagged point.

Holding it to her side, she ran after Wolf-Corey. If she had to, she would use it.

She followed their footprints deeper into the woods. The prints arced around to the left. Soon she found herself heading into the setting sun, toward another clearing. As Leila got closer, she spotted the brown wolf's rear end. The animal had stopped.

As she approached slowly, raising her weapon, she heard a wet, smacking sound. Rhythmic. Like chewing.

She stopped at the edge of the clearing. The brown wolf was feeding, tearing into freshly killed prey.

All Leila caught was a glimpse of silver fur and gleaming red.

She had to turn away. Her vision swirled and she sank to her knees. She felt no danger for herself anymore. The wolf didn't care about her. It had made its conquest.

Its conquest was Corey.

21

Leila felt nauseated. Corey had done this for her. Sacrificed himself, to distract the wolf. To save her. And now he'd paid the price.

This was not what was supposed to happen!

A scream welled up from deep inside. She tried to hold it back, but the anger was like a fist inside her. She felt her hand clench around the metal shard. She didn't care anymore. There was nothing left to lose.

She could behave like an animal, too.

Standing, she turned to face the creature. Raising the improvised weapon over her head, she cried out, "Coreeeeey!"

"What?"

She froze.

From her right, Wolf-Corey emerged from the trees. Leila's arm dropped. "Wait. I thought—isn't that—?"

"You thought Junior was eating me?" Wolf-Corey laughed. "Look at me. I'm a skinny, ugly mess. Would any wolf want this?"

"Then what is it eating?"

"I don't know," Wolf-Corey said. "It tastes like chicken. I started on it. That's why I knew it was here."

"That's disgusting."

"Well, I couldn't find you after we hopped. I went looking, but the snow was really bad. I got totally lost, and I started feeling really weak. When I saw this creature—muskrat, possum, giant rat, I don't know—I got all wolfy and—"

"I don't need to hear the rest."

"Sorry."

"But I want to hug you," Leila said, feeling overcome with relief.

"Don't." Wolf-Corey eyed the other wolf. "Let's get out of that thing's sight. I don't want to die here. This was your idea, coming back to this forest. I didn't want to do it. I wanted to stay in the present."

"But you were the one who grabbed the cigarette case!"

"To save you from those freaks. Come on, let's just go!"

He and Leila took off, deeper into the woods. The farther they got, the slower Wolf-Corey seemed to get. "Are you feeling okay?" Leila asked.

"It comes and goes."

"I don't think we have much time. I saw you—the original human you—and your great-uncle Stanislaw. You passed the hut where I was hiding. Stanislaw didn't look too good."

Wolf-Corey stopped. "Yeah. He'd been beat up by this Nazi creep named Heinrich, just before the forced march. The place where I first met Stanislaw? It was a shack, but not this one. It was where he hid from the Nazi soldiers. We kind of scared each other. But we had to shut up, because while we were inside Heinrich came to pee against the shack. He didn't know we were there. Stanislaw managed to ambush him. I thought he'd kill the guy, but Stanislaw isn't a murderer. He just gave ol' Heinie a really bad head injury to match his. Anyway, that's why he looked so bad. Come." Wolf-Corey loped away, leading Leila deeper into the forest.

"Where are we going?"

"Back to the hut you were talking about. I totally

know which one it is. After that fight with Heinrich, Stanislaw and I fled. He had a map. A secret path through the woods to Kurtstadt. The hut was one of our landmarks." Wolf-Corey squinted into the sun. "Once we get there, we'll follow their steps. He and I—I mean, the human me—we should be heading into a valley pretty soon. Stanislaw gets really weak. He's losing blood now. I have to practically carry him up the hill."

"What's our plan? We can't let Stanislaw meet your grandmother, right? But we can't let him die either!"

"Right. I've been thinking about this," Wolf-Corey said as they wound their way through the trees. "Remember, I know what's about to happen. So. We get caught in a Nazi attack. I save Stanislaw's life. We meet Hitler, in an unmarked car just outside the village of Kurtstadt. Turns out—surprise!—the Allies had occupied the village, and they're waiting to ambush the Nazis. It gets complicated, but when the smoke clears, the Allies win, yay! But Hitler escapes, boo. Stanislaw is taken to a hospital. I'm with him when his sister walks in. I see my grandmother—my mutti—but she's a girl! Her name is Helga. She had been brought there by another Allied rescue mission. When she saw her brother's name on a list of patients, she asked to visit him. And now here she is."

Leila nodded. The wind was picking up, and she drew her coat tighter around her. "She was scheduled to be shipped off to South America, right?" she asked. "But now that Stanislaw was alive, she didn't go. So she never married your grandpa and they never had your mom, and you were never born."

"Exactly."

"So how can you possibly let Human-Corey take Stanislaw to that hospital? The same thing will happen again!"

"This is where I need your help. You have to talk to me—I mean, the old me. Human-Corey."

"HC," Leila suggested.

"Okay, you tell HC what's about to happen to him. Seeing you will be a big deal. Just the fact that you came back from the present—you wouldn't do that unless it was important. He'll get that. Tell him to give the hospital a fake name for Stanislaw—I don't know . . . call him Uncle Fritz. Fritz Einstein."

"Einstein?"

"It's the only German name I know."

Leila thought for a moment. Her family was German. She could read and speak German. She knew plenty of German last names on both sides of the family. "Try Huberman. That's more believable."

"Fine," Wolf-Corey said. "Stanislaw won't be able to correct them. He'll be unconscious for a long time. He won't have any idea. When the Allies bring Helga to the hospital, she'll see the list of other rescued prisoners. But she won't see the name Stanislaw Meyer. She'll see 'Fritz Huberman' but that will be a random name that means nothing to her. So she won't have any reason to stop off and see him. Off she goes to South America, where eventually she meets my grandfather."

"Right . . ." Leila nodded. "Meanwhile old Stanislaw heals in the hospital. Maybe later he notices they made a mistake with his name, but it seems like a silly thing. The doctors correct it, and ha ha ha, everyone has a laugh. But Helga is already on her way to South America, where she will fall in love with your grandfather. Years later, Corey is born."

"The chaos loop is unlooped," Wolf-Corey agreed. "Everybody wins."

"Brilliant."

"I know."

The wind was shrieking now, whipping the snow into Leila's face. As they reached the hut, Wolf-Corey stopped.

"There's one problem with that plan," Leila said, stopping with him.

"What?"

"I'm not a Throwback, remember? I can't get HC to change history. You have to tell him."

"I'm a wolf."

"He's *you*, Corey. He knows about transspeciation. He knows Smig. I'll explain things to him. He'll get it."

"There's another problem," Wolf-Corey said, sniffing the air.

Leila looked over the landscape. Just past the building, the snow was blowing upward into swirling white spirals.

Human-Corey's and Stanislaw's footprints were gone.

22

"Ohhhh, great," Wolf-Corey moaned.

"Yup." Leila scanned the swirling snow cover for any sign of footprints. The sun was nearly touching the horizon and the air seemed to be getting colder by the second. "What do we do now?"

"Do you have some ibuprofen?"

Leila looked at him. "Corey, we're stuck."

"We're not," he said. "I can get us there. Remember, I did this before. It just hurts."

"What hurts?"

"Everything. My head, my legs, my stomach. I'm not feeling too good." He began stepping quickly away from the hut. "But, hey, I'll suck it up. Like I said, it comes and goes."

Leila watched him for a second or two. He was limping. His fur was matted. In spots, his skin showed through. "I'm worried about you."

"Indigestion," he said. "I think the muskrat needed ketchup."

He seemed to know where he was going, so she followed. As he wound his way through the trees, everything looked the same to Leila. But Wolf-Corey moved in a slow, deliberate zigzag pattern, stopping every once in a while to sniff the air.

It was nearly dark when they got to a road. The snow had blown off parts of it, leaving a scrubby strip of pebbles and dead grass. Thick, brambly bushes rose up on either side, but Leila could make out fresh tire prints thinly covered with snow.

She smiled. A dirt road meant civilization was nearby. "Some convoy came through here, right? It was a bunch of Nazi vehicles that the Allies had stolen. You knew from your family history that Stanislaw was going to make a fatal mistake. He would think they were real Nazis and shoot at them. And they would kill him. That's why you hopped. You saved his life from that. Did I get that right?"

Wolf-Corey lay down on his stomach. His chest was heaving in and out. Leila could see his ribs. "Yeah, that's what I did," he said.

"Corey, you don't have indigestion," Leila said, "and it's not coming and going. You're really sick."

She moved toward him, but he growled.

As she backed away, he exhaled. "Sorry. I didn't mean that. But that road—it isn't the same one that the convoy used. This one is way too narrow. And too flat."

"But I'm thinking we should follow it anyway," Leila said cautiously, "because any road out here would lead to that Allied-occupied village. . . ."

"It's called Kurtstadt," Wolf-Corey said. "And, yeah, you're probably right. Unless there's some other village nearby."

"So which direction do we take?"

But Wolf-Corey was staring off to the left, away from the road. He stood and walked in that direction on shaky legs. "Walk this way."

Leila squinted. Maybe fifty yards ahead was a patch of dull amber, a place where the sun was casting its last rays on snow. "That's not the road. Where are you going?"

"See the bottom of that hill?" he replied. "I'm pretty sure that's the one where Stanislaw almost collapsed. I practically had to carry him up."

"How sure is pretty sure?" Leila asked.

"Let me run over and check," Wolf-Corey replied. "Stay here. I'll come back. I'm faster than you, even in this state. I don't want to waste time if I'm wrong."

He was having trouble getting back on his feet, so Leila leaned over to help. "You're faster than me? Really? Maybe I should go instead."

As she wrapped her arms around his chest, Wolf-Corey let out a pained squeal and snapped at her arm.

Leila jumped back. "Hey, watch it!"

Grrrrrrr . . .

His eyes had lost their brightness. They were cold and bloodshot. He trembled as he stood. Without saying a word, without acknowledging Leila at all, he turned and began loping away.

Leila stood still. She watched as he staggered onward, slowly picking up speed. She wasn't sure what to do.

The wind whistled softly, blowing snow from the tree canopies. In the distance, Leila heard another howl. She shuddered, but it was so far away, it didn't really scare her.

The rustling of the bushes behind her did.

Leila snapped her head around. The bushes were thick with snow. Nothing seemed to be moving. "Hello?" she called out.

On the other side of the road, something moved high in the branches of a pine tree. She watched a clump of snow shake loose and fall to the ground with a dull thump. Leila took a deep breath.

Take it easy, she told herself. *Stay calm and sit tight.*

She turned back around. Wolf-Corey had disappeared down a slope. He was probably heading to the bottom of the hill. She counted to one hundred, hoping he'd return. But she couldn't hear him. And she couldn't see Human-Corey and Stanislaw, who were supposed to be approaching.

What if Wolf-Corey spotted himself and his uncle? Would he actually remember to return for Leila? That was the plan. They could only do this together. But she was worried about Wolf-Corey's health. And his mental state.

Flashes of deep orange shone through the branches to the west. In moments the sun would be below the horizon. She glanced upward, but it was impossible to see a moon through the trees. When it was dark, going after Wolf-Corey might be impossible. Even the whiteness of the snow wouldn't be much help. In that case she'd have to turn back to the road and follow it, without him.

But she didn't want to do this alone.

Cautiously she stepped forward. "Pssst!" she called out. "Hey, Corey? Can you hear me?"

She followed his footprints through a wide corridor of snow flanked on either side by bushes. The ground angled upward until she arrived at the top of a long, gradual decline.

Wolf-Corey was lying down on his stomach, half-way to the bottom. She could hear him wheezing.

Ahead of him was a valley. To the right, a steep hill rose from the bottom of the valley toward the approaching night sky. This must have been the hill he had climbed with his great-uncle.

Leila squinted at the dull brightness coming from beyond the top of the hill. It wasn't just the last hint of sun. There were clusters of different-colored light—white and yellow and uneven.

Kurtstadt.

It was impossible to tell how far. But there were no footsteps on the hill, which meant the climb hadn't happened yet.

Wolf-Corey was waiting.

"Hey! Pssst! You said you were going to get me," she whispered, hoping he would hear her.

He didn't, so she stepped forward, heading down the slope toward him.

The bushes rustled again. "*Hallo*," said a voice.

Leila leaped away. She lost her balance and nearly fell.

A shadow slid out from the bushes. It was a man, maybe six feet tall. He was wearing a helmet and a uniform. As he stepped toward her, he limped badly. On his shoulder, barely visible in the growing darkness, was a swastika.

"*Mir ist kalt*," he said, moving closer.

I'm cold.

23

"*M*ir ist auch kalt," Leila replied. *I'm cold, too.*
It was the only thing she could think to say.
The man cocked his head. He took off his helmet
and bowed low. The politeness seemed weird and
creepy here in the woods. Leila looked around for a
path of escape. But now he was indicating the top of
his head with his free hand. He was bowing because he
wanted her to see something there. "*Siehst du, was sie mir
angetan haben?*" *Do you see what they did to me?*

Leila narrowed her eyes. The man's head was swollen. Blood had seeped through his hair and frozen
against the side of his face. "*Das ist schrecklich,*" she said.
That is terrible.

She glanced down into the valley. Wolf-Corey was

unmoving. Too far away to hear any of this.

As the Nazi soldier stood, his eyes bore into Leila's. He followed her glance down the hill. "*Ach. Wolf.*"

Leila lurched away from him and began to run. But the man's reflexes were quick. He leaped after her and gripped her arm.

"Cor—" she shouted.

He shoved his free hand over her mouth and pulled her into the bushes. "*Sei ruhig! Diese Tiere sind wild. Sie werden uns lebendig essen! Ich habe eine Pistole. Ich werde sie benutzen, um uns zu beschützen.*"

Be quiet! These animals are savage. They will eat us alive. I have a gun. I will use it to protect us.

Leila struggled against his grip, but she felt something pressed against her back. "*Bitte, lass mich in Ruhe, und lass den Wolf in Ruhe. Er ist krank. Er wird uns nicht schaden,*" she pleaded.

Please, leave me alone, and leave the wolf alone. It is sick. It won't harm us.

"*Dein Akzent,*" he growled. "*Bist du Amerikanisch?*"

Your accent. You are American?

"*Nein!*" Leila cried out. If he thought she was the enemy, he'd kill her.

The man let go of her. As she spun around to face him, she saw that he had been pressing into her back the butt end of a pocketknife, not a gun.

"*Hab keine Angst. Ich töte keine hilflosen amerikanischen Mädchen*," the man said with a grin, shoving the pocket-knife back into his pocket. "*Vor allem, wenn sie mir von einem amerikanischen Jungen erzählen können, der mit einem Polen namens Stanislaw entkommen ist? Hmm? Dieses Schwein hat versucht mich zu töten!*"

Don't be afraid. I do not kill helpless American girls. Especially if they can tell me about an American boy who escaped with a Pole named Stanislaw? Hmm? That pig tried to kill me!

Leila swallowed hard. He suspected her. Of course. What were the chances of running into two thirteen-year-old Americans in the woods?

Corey's story replayed in her mind—Corey arriving into this forest . . . meeting Stanislaw in a shack where he hid from a death march . . . a fight with a Nazi captor. . . .

"What's your name?" she blurted out. "I mean, *Wie heißen Sie?*"

"Schmauder," he replied. "Heinrich Schmauder."

Heinrich.

It was a common name. The German equivalent of Henry.

But it was also the name of the Nazi who had beaten Stanislaw. *I thought he'd kill the guy,* Corey had said, but Stanislaw isn't a murderer. He just gave ol' Heinie a really bad head injury to match his.

A head injury like the one this guy had.

"He spared your life," Leila said. "You tortured him. And when he had you, he could have killed you. But he showed mercy. And now you're coming to finish him off?"

Heinrich cocked his head in confusion. "Wie bitte?"

Out of the corner of her eye, Leila could see Wolf-Corey struggling to his feet, heading toward the bottom of the hill. Away from them. He must have seen something. Maybe Human-Corey and Stanislaw were approaching.

If Wolf-Corey was seeing them, then Heinrich would, too.

"Dieser Amerikanische Junge ist mein Bruder!" she blurted. "Stanislaw ist ein . . . Entführer! Sie fahren nach Kurtstadt. Ich kenne einen Kurzweg. Kommen Sie."

This American boy is my brother! Stanislaw is a kidnapper! They are heading for Kurtstadt. I know a shortcut. Come!

The excuse sounded so fake. She prayed it would work. Heinrich was eyeing her suspiciously.

She had to act fast. She needed to get him away. Turning toward the road, she began walking as fast as she could.

Heinrich did not protest. Instead he followed her.

Before long she heard a trickle of water. A river, deep and lined with boulders, angled in from in the forest. It took a sharp curve, following alongside the road. Water gurgled through breaks in the ice. Ahead, Leila could make out the dull glow of the lights from the village.

"*Ah, Kurtstadt, gut, danke,*" Heinrich said, casting her a cold glance. "*Bleiben bei mir. Die Soldaten werden sich freuen, dich zu sehen.*"

Good, thank you. You will stay with me. The soldiers will be happy to see you.

His voice was chilling. He thought he was leading her into Nazi arms. He probably expected a hero's welcome for delivering an American.

He had no clue the village had been taken over by the Allies.

If Leila stayed with him, Heinrich would be in for a shock. He'd be taken prisoner. She could go straight to the hospital and carry out her plan with Corey.

They trudged silently for what felt like a long time. Heinrich was breathing heavily, grimacing, holding on to his head injury. But the lights didn't seem to be getting any closer. The village was farther than it seemed, an optical illusion of the wintry night. Finally Heinrich stopped. "*Ich bin durstig*," he announced.

I'm thirsty.

Leila nodded. The sound of the water was tempting. The river was meandering away from the road, and this might be the last chance they had.

Heinrich let Leila go first down the slope to the riverbank. The wind rustled the leaves and blew a chunk of loose snow onto her head. She stopped, wiping her jacket clean.

A few steps behind her, Heinrich had stopped, too. He lifted a finger to his lips. A silent *sssssh*.

Then, slowly, he pointed to a spot farther along the river. There, set back from the water about six feet, was an enormous rock outcropping. Heinrich walked past her, heading toward the rock, signaling Leila to stay put.

Instead she stepped forward, following him quietly. As she got closer, she could make out sets of fresh footprints, leading from the other side of the rock right down to the river edge.

Someone was hiding.

Or someones.

Leila's mind raced. If these people felt the need to hide, they were escaping something. If they were escaping something, that something would be Nazis.

Heinrich was the last person they'd want to see.

She had to warn them. Without getting Heinrich angry enough to retaliate.

Putting her foot down on a rock, she pretended to slip. As she fell to the ground, she let out a cry of "Oops!"

Loud.

Heinrich froze, still facing the big rock. He crouched low, taking the knife from his pocket. Leila heard a *ssshhhick* sound as he flipped the blade open.

From out behind the rock came a thin young man. He wore a dark cap, a woolen coat, and thick boots. A gun hung from a holster on his black belt.

As he stepped slowly and deliberately toward Heinrich, he raised one hand in a stiff salute.

"*Heil Hitler*," he barked.

Heinrich lowered the knife, flipping the blade back into its case. "*Gott sei Dank*," he murmured. *Thank God*.

Then he snapped to attention, clicked his heels, and shouted back in a loud, robust voice:

"*Heil Hitler!*"

24

Leila backed away. The two men were hugging now. The only thing worse than a Nazi murderer was two Nazi murderers. They were so smug. Once they got to Kurtstadt they would find the surprise of their lives.

But there were more important things to think about. She needed to get there first. Before Corey and Stanislaw did.

The two men were ignoring her. She ducked behind trees and inched away quietly, praying they wouldn't see. The snow had seeped through her boots now, making her socks wet, weighing down her steps.

The sound of a gunshot made her stumble.

She leaped behind a tree just thick enough to hide

her. Had they seen her? Were they headed this way?

Leila braced to run. But there was a commotion now—other voices, not just two. Carefully she peered out from behind the trunk. Heinrich and the other soldier were no longer alone. A group of people had come out from behind the rock. They crowded around the two men. Fists were flying. The air filled with muffled shouts and curses. Leila couldn't tell what was going on, but it didn't matter. She was safe now. She had a clear path to Kurtstadt.

But what she saw made her jaw drop.

The other people were not soldiers at all. They were dressed in threadbare coats, their heads covered with rags. As their coats flapped open, she caught glimpses of the vertical stripes on their shirts and pants.

The stripes meant they were concentration camp prisoners. They were escapees.

How were they able to overpower two Nazi soldiers?

In the midst of the crowd she could see both Heinrich and the other soldier. But they weren't fighting the prisoners. They were fighting each other.

Now it all made sense. The other guy wasn't a soldier at all. He had been in disguise. The "Heil Hitler" was fake.

This was an ambush. They were all attacking Heinrich.

One of the prisoners, a gaunt man who could have been ninety, doddered toward the fight with a branch held high. A moment later he was hurtling to the ground, screaming. The stick went flying into the snow. No one seemed to have noticed.

Leila backed away. She didn't have time for this. But the old man was lying motionless. Heinrich was fighting the others back, hard. He was strong and ruthless. These people were starved, cold, and weak. They weren't going to live long in this weather. They needed to reach safety.

Did they know about Kurtstadt? If she joined in now, if she helped them overpower Heinrich, they could all march there together. The Allies would welcome them.

She looked back toward the village lights. It would take Corey and Stanislaw a while to get there. Stanislaw would be going slowly.

She would have some time.

Running out from behind the rock, she ran to the old man. He was still breathing, and she roused him. Glancing up at her dazedly, he muttered a confused "*Danke.*"

Thanks.

She grabbed his dropped branch and headed toward the melee.

Heinrich was struggling. Three of the prisoners were beating him with their fists. The disguised Nazi soldier had a holstered gun, but he wasn't using it now. Instead of shooting Heinrich, he was drawing a rope from a pack. As Leila got closer, Heinrich's eyes caught her approaching.

"NAZI!" he yelled at the top of his lungs. "HIER KOMMT EIN NAZI!"

Here comes a Nazi.

Heads turned. It was enough of a distraction for Heinrich to break loose. He grabbed the pistol from the guard's belt, spun, and took a prisoner by the neck. It was a young, dark-haired woman not much older than Leila, with a birthmark on her right cheek. She looked terrified, her fists pounding against Heinrich's arm. "*Einen Schritt näher und ich erschiesse sie!*" Heinrich shrieked.

One step closer and I'll shoot her!

He backed up the slope, pointing the gun at the prisoner's head. The others stood still, helpless. Leila could see that the disguised Nazi guard had a second holster on his belt. He was trying to reach for it without Heinrich noticing.

No such luck.

Heinrich jammed the gun into the young woman's forehead, and she screamed. "*Hände hoch!*" Heinrich shouted down to the prisoners.

Hands high.

The others had no choice now. They meekly raised their hands as Heinrich tightened his hold on his prey, choking her. She struggled to get loose as he yanked her backward and up the hill.

Leila set her jaw. He was not going to do to that girl what he'd done to Stanislaw. "Oh no you don't," she murmured.

She broke for the hill, but not directly at Heinrich. Instead she ran upward, parallel to Heinrich's path, forcing him to look away from the prisoners.

"*Bleib stehen!*" Heinrich shouted, pointing his gun toward Leila. *Stay right there!*

A shot rang out from the small crowd below. Someone had used the moment to grab a gun. The shot went up into the air. It was meant only to scare Heinrich.

The distraction was perfect.

Throwing her stick aside, Leila darted left toward the Nazi. She put her head down, took five or six strong running steps, and leaped at his legs.

Her shoulder made contact with his knees. Or maybe it was the prisoner's knees. She couldn't tell. All she knew was that both of them tumbled into the snow. Heinrich cursed in German, and his gun flew from his hands. As it landed in the snow three feet away, the prisoner lunged for it.

Heinrich scrabbled to his feet and went after the gun, too. From below, the others stormed up the hill toward them. Leila fell back, a sharp pain shooting through her shoulder and head. She tried to make out what was happening but it was total pandemonium. A mass of flying fists and legs all tumbled down the hill toward the river.

She sat up, grimacing. Another shot rang out, and then another.

After the second, the noise abruptly stopped. A puff of black smoke rose into the skies. The small group, murmuring, backed away toward the river.

A body remained in the snow, facedown.

Leila stood and walked toward it. The young woman Heinrich had captured was standing over the body, the gun smoldering in her hand. She was crying.

As Leila came near, she looked up and nodded. "*Danke*," she said softly. "*Und Gott vergib mir.*"

Thank you. And may God forgive me.

She dropped the gun into the snow, near the body. The man who had disguised himself as a Nazi soldier flipped the body on its back.

Heinrich's lifeless face looked up into the white sky.

One of the prisoners began chanting a prayer, but another shook his head angrily and spat on the corpse.

Leila looked away. *"Kennen Sie Kurtstadt?"* she asked the disguised Nazi soldier. *Do you know about Kurtstadt?*

Before answering, he ripped the swastika from his arm and threw it on Heinrich's body. *"Ja. Da sind Verbündete. Ich bin mit dem Widerstand."* He smiled. *"Und jetzt bist du auch bei uns."*

Yes. Allies are there. I am part of the Resistance. And now you are with us, too.

Leila nodded. *"Ich heiße Leila,"* she said. *My name is Leila.*

"Martin," the man replied.

He explained that they had been marching for days, and that they had already lost two people to starvation.

He leaned over Heinrich's body and turned it back around, facedown into the snow. Then with a nod, he walked away from it.

All of them began trudging along the river toward

Kurtstadt, murmuring, sobbing quietly. Many of them looked drained and expressionless. Leila fell in beside the young woman with the birthmark.

No one seemed to have the energy to talk. Their footsteps crunched softly in the snow, as the lights of the distant village beckoned.

PART III
Corey

25

Wolf-Corey sat for a very long time at the side of the valley. He knew he should have turned back to find Leila. But he couldn't move.

His eyes were locked on a rabbit. It was fat, scampering in and out of the bushes, looking for berries. Or whatever rabbits looked for.

All he had to do was sit still. Sit still and not move. When the rabbit turned away from him, when its eyes were angled in the other direction—then he would pounce.

His stomach let out a soft growl. He was hungry.

There.

He didn't know how he knew the right time to attack. But it was the right time.

Corey sprang toward the unsuspecting creature. But his legs gave way beneath him and he stumbled in the snow.

The rabbit, hearing something, whipped its head back around. Corey saw its two black eyes for a moment. He saw its whiskers twitch.

And then it was gone. Blended in with the snow.

Arrrrrghhhh!

Cursing his own clumsiness, Wolf-Corey stood and shook himself off. He limped toward his prey, but it was long gone.

Some wolf.

Now his legs made a weird *crick-crick-crick* as he walked. He felt tired. Bone-tired. His mind was blanking out and then back in again.

This was not normal. And it wasn't just indigestion or fatigue. Leila had sensed something was very, very wrong. It had been dumb to leave her. Dumb to promise he'd scout out the area and report back to her. She should have come with him. He missed her. And now he was too burned-out to go back to her.

He turned to look behind him. Where was she?

Corey knew exactly where *he* was. The valley below was the place he and Stanislaw had found on the way to Kurtstadt. He felt it in his bones. He recognized the steep hill that led upward to the village, to his right. He recognized the part of the forest, to his left, where they'd emerged after escaping Heinrich.

The valley was free of footprints. Which meant Human-Corey and Stanislaw hadn't arrived yet. This was the chance. He and Leila could put their plan into action—stop them and talk to them. Convince them to change Stanislaw's name on the hospital intake sheet.

"Leila!" he called out, in a voice so weak even he could barely hear it.

Suck it up and do it, he told himself.

As he turned back, he saw another movement in the woods. Something distant and large.

His chest pounded with hunger pangs. Maybe this was a bear. Were there bears in the German forest?

Wolf-Corey moved behind a bush, out of sight. He stood stock-still, angling his body toward the movement. It was two figures, and they weren't bears. They crashed through the underbrush, one tall and skinny, the other slightly shorter and broad.

Himself and Great-Uncle Stanislaw. In the flesh.

"Come on, Stan."

At the sound of his own voice, Wolf-Corey barely suppressed a whimper of longing. He hated hearing his own wolf whimpers. Instead he silently watched himself, as a human, walk out of the woods. His arm was wrapped around his great-uncle's shoulder, as the older man stumbled forward on shaky legs. "You can do this," said Human-Corey. "The valley is our last landmark before the river. And you know what comes after the river, right?"

"*Ja*," Great-Uncle Stanislaw replied. "Wiener schnitzel."

"No, Kurtstadt!" his human self said. "Remember Kurtstadt?"

"Ah! So sorry. I was dreaming . . . about dinner. Isn't that funny, dreaming while standing up?"

Wolf-Corey remembered the conversation. Stanislaw was weak, on the verge of collapse. As the two walked through the valley, Wolf-Corey looked over his shoulder. He prayed Leila was hearing this.

He needed her right now.

The two struggled across the flat, snowy plain, then began climbing the hill. Stanislaw's knees buckled, and he nearly took Human-Corey down with him.

Stanislaw's voice was raspy and weak. "I . . . am afraid . . . you should . . . leave me here."

"Nope," replied Human-Corey. "Out of the question."

"I command you!" Now Stanislaw was pulling away.

"Go. I stay here. I rest. You will find a doctor and come back to me."

Human-Corey resisted his great-uncle, yanking the older man's arm back around his shoulder. "I'm not letting go," he said, "if I have to carry you."

"Ha!" Stanislaw replied. "You are . . . *ein ungewöhnlicher Junge.*"

"You don't have to insult me."

"It means 'an unusual boy.' It is meaning to be a good thing. You are kind. And brave."

"That's what family is all about," Human-Corey replied.

Wolf-Corey came out from behind the bush. Their backs were to him. He wasn't sure what to do. Without Leila to explain, they would be afraid of him. They would run. He wasn't feeling strong right now. His voice was weak, his reflexes slow.

He would have to sneak up pretty close to be heard.

Now Stanislaw's knees were buckling again. This time when he fell, he took Human-Corey with him. Together they tumbled downhill, closer to Wolf-Corey.

They were arguing. Stanislaw was insisting he wanted to die. He was so weak. There was no doubt— if Human-Corey were to leave Stanislaw alone, he'd be toast.

Wolf-Corey's stomach began to rumble. His eyes focused on Stanislaw. The feeling inside him was changing. It was something overwhelming. Impossible to resist.

It was the same feeling that had overcome him when he'd time-hopped into this forest, just hours ago. It had welled up at the sight of that woodland animal. His brain had gone unconscious, but his reflexes had sharpened. In moments, before he could even think about what he was doing, he had trapped it, killed it, and had a feast.

It was a hunger that reached inside and nuked everything else. A hunger that made any live thing look like food. Even an injured, nearly dead, middle-aged man.

How can you even be thinking about this? screamed the voice of the old Corey. *He is your own ancestor!*

But that part of his brain was no longer in control. It was shrinking by the nanosecond. He fought the urge to sprint after them, to hunt them down. Instead he walked, trying as hard as he could to tamp down the instinct. To be rational. To stick to a plan. He saw Human-Corey turn.

And now he was facing . . . himself. And himself looked impossibly afraid.

Wolf-Corey threw his head back to shout a greeting,

but all that came out was a howl.

And that was when he remembered:

He had been here before.

When he'd been human, when he'd been here with Stanislaw, he had seen a wolf. This scene, right now, had played out exactly the same way, only the Corey roles had been reversed.

So he knew what was about to happen. Stanislaw, who was afraid of wolves, would panic. The panic would give him a jolt of energy. He and Human-Corey would make it to the top of the hill. And they'd go on to Kurtstadt. They'd live, but they'd prevent Corey from being born.

But it didn't have to be that way. He could change everything now. Make it all work out. With or without Leila.

She wasn't the Throwback, *he* was.

He began to run. Human-Corey's eyes widened. He said exactly the thing he had said before. "D-d-d-does it attack humans?"

"I don't know!" Stanislaw replied. "Maybe it's trying to tell us something. But I do not want to find out! I am very much afraid of wolves." He was shaking, trying to reach into his own jacket. "The gun. Use Heinrich's gun!"

Wolf-Corey picked up speed. Corey was pulling the gun out of Stanislaw's jacket, fumbling with it. "I don't know how to use it!"

"*Just shoot it!*" Stanislaw said.

It wasn't going to work, he knew this. Human-Corey was going to shoot wild and miss.

Now. Speak. They will hear you now.

Change it. Change everything!

As Wolf-Corey opened his mouth, the pair screamed in fear. Human-Corey lifted the gun and shot.

CRRRRRACK!

Wolf-Corey stopped in his tracks.

It hurt.

He hadn't remembered it this way. He remembered missing the wolf. He remembered the wolf stopping in midleap and sitting on its haunches. He had thought the wolf was stunned by the noise. Dumbfounded.

But it wasn't that at all.

The bullet hurt like crazy. It had torn his right leg. He tried to lunge forward, but the leg just wasn't working.

He opened his mouth but no sound came out. Human-Corey and Stanislaw were running now. To the top of the hill. They'd continue onward to Kurtstadt.

Everything had gone exactly the same.

They would do the things they had done before. And Corey would never be born.

Corey felt himself dropping into the snow. It felt somehow warm and comforting. It was a beautiful deep red where his leg was bleeding out. He was tired, so tired.

As his vision blurred, he could only think of one thing.

He'd jumped into the chaos loop. And the chaos loop had won.

PART IV
Leila

26

Leila was nervous. The going was way slower than she wanted. The sun had set, so they had to plot their course by the moonlight's reflection on the snow and the lights of Kurtstadt. The prisoners had tattered shoes and threadbare clothing. Two or three of them coughed uncontrollably. One of the women was pregnant. Martin had a backpack stocked with bandages, aspirin, iodine, and random other equipment, but it wasn't anywhere near enough.

She worried about Corey. By now he would have found his human self and Stanislaw. She hoped he'd talked to them. She hoped they were all heading for safety.

There was strength in numbers.

She walked with the old man, the one who'd tried to attack Heinrich with a stick. When he collapsed in the snow, Leila lifted him. He weighed less than she did and could barely walk, so she propped him up to keep going. He kept muttering *Let me die* in German, over and over, but no one was going to do that.

But there was something else that no one was going to do—hurry.

By the fifth time they'd stopped, Leila knew that staying with these people was not going to work. Time was running out. She had to break loose and get to Kurtstadt on her own. As slow as Stanislaw and Human-Corey would be going, it couldn't possibly be slower than this.

"*Bitte*," Leila began. "*Ich muss*—"

But before she could say *Please, I must go*, she heard an eruption of gunfire directly ahead. They all fell silent, looking toward Kurtstadt. A moment later an explosion rang out. Then another. Black-gray smoke rose upward, obscuring the lights of the village.

Leila's heart sank. The fighting, she realized, had begun. If they'd arrived when they were supposed to, Stanislaw and Human-Corey would be involved in this. Stanislaw would be shot, and Human-Corey would be getting him to the hospital.

Were they there already? On their way? Was Wolf-Corey with them? She needed to get there to find out. Now.

"*Was passiert?*" murmured Martin. *What is happening?*

Leila took a deep breath. She explained that the village was under Nazi attack.

"*Meine Leute . . . wie kann ich sie dorthin bringen?*" Martin said, looking toward the ragtag group.

My people . . . how can I bring them there?

Their faces were gaunt and fearful, their eyes hollow. Leila knew they'd be risking their lives to go anywhere near this fighting.

"*Können Sie woanders hingehen?*" Leila pressed.

Is there another place you can go?

The young woman Leila had saved murmured something to the soldier, who took a map from his jacket pocket. Together they examined it for a few moments, tracing their fingers here and there. Finally Martin nodded. "*Ja,*" he said. "*Es gibt ein anderes freundliches Dorf, namens Kreuzung, vielleicht fünf Kilometer nördlich. Ich denke, wir können es erreichen.*"

Yes, there is another friendly village called Kreuzung about three miles north. I think we can reach that.

"*Gut! Gehen Sie dorthin,*" Leila said.

Good. Go there.

"*Und du?*" Martin asked.

And you?

Leila didn't know what to say. Lying didn't seem right, but the truth was too bizarre to admit. "*Ich muss nach Kurtstadt,*" she said, "*um jemandem zu helfen.*"

I must go to Kurtstadt to help someone.

Martin nodded. "*Dies muss jemand sein, den du sehr liebst.*"

This must be someone you love very much.

Leila wasn't expecting the rush of blood to her face. "*Ja,*" she said softly.

Martin nodded silently. He wished her good luck and Godspeed.

Leila spun away. But she hadn't gone two steps before she heard an urgent voice cry out, "*Warte mal!*"

Wait a minute.

She turned back. The young woman she had saved approached her with a silver chain. Hanging from it was a fancy silver Star of David. She smiled, her birthmark disappearing into a deep dimple on her cheek.

She lifted the chain high. As Leila bowed her head, the woman slipped it around her neck. "*Diese Kette wird dir Glück bringen. Geh mit unserem Segen.*"

This necklace will bring you luck. Go with our blessing.

Leila gave her a hug. She was barely more than skin and bones. For a moment, Leila thought she might crush her. But the woman's grip was steely and stubborn.

As Leila turned and sprinted in the direction of Kurtstadt, she felt an electric surge of strength.

When she got there, Kurtstadt was a war zone.

Leila couldn't see the buildings through a haze of smoke. She heard the whining of car engines and the rumble of trucks. But she could catch only glimpses of the convoy. It had entered the area from a sloped road in the other direction. Helmeted men in long, wool coats dropped to their knees and fired toward the center of the skirmish.

She stayed low to the ground, scanning the area. She knew what was supposed to be happening now. According to Corey's description, he and Stanislaw had reached the village just before the fighting began. They had survived it somehow.

Leila tried to identify them. But at this distance, with the smoke and flying debris, it was impossible to make out faces.

It would be insane to try to get closer. She backed away, toward the cover of the surrounding forest. A stray bullet ripped a chunk off a pine tree to her right. Shards of wood shot toward her, and she flinched, retreating farther.

Leila realized her best bet would be to lie low and wait this out. After the fighting stopped, she could make her way to the hospital. If all had gone according to plan, Human-Corey would be there along with Wolf-Corey and Stanislaw. They'd have already changed Stanislaw's name on the hospital records.

She hoped.

Leila backed away. But deeper into the forest meant less snow, and less snow meant darkness. The dark scared her. Through the trees to her left, she noticed a wash of brightness. Some kind of clearing, maybe.

As she approached, she could make out a broad stretch of snowy ground. It sloped gently downward to the left, away from Kurtstadt. As she walked, her footsteps crunched on the snow-flecked forest floor. She lifted her feet and placed them as softly as she could.

But at the sound of a sudden explosion, she jumped.

The noise set the dogs in the village howling. It lit up the entire clearing in a sickening bluish white, like a giant carpet through the center of the forest.

This carpet—was it the path Corey and Stanislaw had taken toward the village?

She walked faster, but something rustled in the trees above her. A large bird with a long neck and crooked beak had just taken off into the air from a branch. It soared upward, circling in the moonlight with three others just like it.

Vultures.

Vultures ate carrion. Dead creatures. They sensed death. They hovered above their prey, swooping down for dinner if the prey was dead. If the prey wasn't quite dead yet, they waited. These were waiting. For something or someone.

She hoped they weren't waiting for her.

Another explosion lit up the sky. This time, among the distant dog howls, she heard something nearer. It came from her left, down the wide slope.

It was a low, deep growl.

Leila moved closer. She peeked around the trees and saw a dark mass in the snow. From this distance she couldn't tell what it was. But the vultures were directly above it.

One of the big birds landed on the ground nearby. But the shape moved. It was alive. The vulture, frustrated, hopped away and then took flight again.

When she heard the thing growl again, louder, Leila knew what it was.

She raced through the trees toward it. She could see a flash of teeth now, a stuttering walk, a mass of fur trailing blood behind it.

Silver-gray fur.

"Corey!" she cried.

Now Leila was out in the open, racing down the slope as fast as she could. She paid no attention to the static of the gunfire behind her. It was distant, from Kurtstadt, which felt light-years away right now.

Corey was barely able to move. He didn't raise his eyes to Leila until she was upon him. "Corey, what happened?" she cried out. "Are you okay?"

In answer, Corey flashed his teeth. His mouth flapped open and shut, as if he were trying to say something.

Leila sat in the snow next to him. She reached out to cup his chin in her hand. She didn't care if he bit her. "Can you speak?"

Corey didn't answer for a long time. When he did, his voice was barely audible. Leila leaned closer, but the words were mumbled, not more than grunts. "Repeat that, Corey . . ."

"I . . ."

His eyes rolled back into his head.

"Keep going," Leila said. "You . . . *what*?"

"Did . . ."

She was losing him. "Corey, hang in there," she said. "Did you see them? Did you talk to them? What happened? You did *what*?"

Corey's eyes flickered open again. They were dry and bloodshot. A wheeze escaped from his mouth. "Nothing."

"You did nothing? Is that what you're saying?"

"I did . . . nothing . . . Leila."

His head sank to the snow, but Leila lifted it. "It's okay, Corey. Hang in there. We'll go back. We'll get you better. We can try again."

She fumbled in her pocket for her coins. Her cell phone. All the metal she had from the present. As she held them in her right hand, she wrapped her left arm around Corey. His heart was beating, but barely. "Come on . . ." she said through gritted teeth.

As a shadow passed over them, she looked up. A vulture descended, its wings spread wide. On either side, its feathers looked like greedy, outstretched fingers.

27

"Ow! Those are my fingers!"

The voice startled Leila. She felt her eyes flutter. She felt pummeled. Like she'd been taken apart and put together. Which meant she'd just time-hopped.

And as the memories rushed in, she tried to sit up. Where was Corey? She'd been holding him. She'd time-hopped with him. He should have been in her arms. Had someone taken him from her?

"*Corey?*" she blurted.

"No. Gladys." The face of a white-haired woman loomed over her. Her eyes peered out quizzically from under a light-blue Central Park Conservancy volunteer hat. "And you have quite a grip, young lady."

Leila sat up all the way and groaned. Her head felt like it had just spent an hour in a waffle iron. In her dream, she had been battling the vulture's wings, which looked like fingers. She must have attacked poor old Gladys. "Sorry."

"That's all right, dear, I have another hand," the woman said. "Are you feeling okay?"

Leila looked desperately left and right. *Corey.* Where was Corey? "Have you seen a wolf?"

"I beg your pardon?" Gladys said.

The old Central Park blockhouse stood about ten feet away. Which meant the Knickerbocker headquarters was just below her. The artifacts had gotten her back to the present—but they'd missed the original destination by a few feet. Maybe Corey had made it inside. Time travel was so unpredictable.

Was he alive or dead? Could dying Throwbacks make the trip through time?

"I—I must have fallen asleep," Leila said, struggling to stand.

"Dearie, I'm concerned about you," Gladys said. "The walkway is an odd place for a nap. Who is Curly?"

"Corey." Leila had to get inside. But not while anyone was watching. *Why was this person so annoying?* "My friend. He was going to meet me here. He's always late. So I fell asleep. And I had a bad dream. Sorry if I lashed out. I'll be fine. Anyway, bye!"

Gladys shook her head disapprovingly and climbed slowly into a Central Park Conservancy golf cart. "Men. It's always the same. Take my advice—if he's late now, he'll be late the rest of your life."

As she puttered out of sight, Leila raced up to the blockhouse, climbed the steps, and pounded on the door. "Hey! Let me in!"

No way were they going to hear her. She pulled her phone out of her pocket but realized she had never called or texted Bee. She didn't even know Bee's last name.

So she pounded again. And again. Until a family strolled up the hill, looking at her warily. "Howdy!" called out the dad. "You do know that's been closed for, oh, a century or so?"

Leila forced a smile. This place was too public at this hour. She'd have to find another entrance. Philbert had ticked off a list of them. *One is directly out of the subway tunnel along Fifty-Ninth Street. Another in the men's room of the Conservatory Garden. A little hut on Central Park West and 104th, a small electrical substation in the Ramble. Behind a waterfall in the North Woods—*

The waterfall. That was the place where Smig lived. It wasn't too far from here. Leila ran past the family and down the hill to Park Drive.

"Tourists," the dad muttered. "So rude."

She didn't stop running until she had circled out to the road and then back into the North Woods a little farther south. There, under a small wooden bridge, was a gentle waterfall. And in the rocks beneath that waterfall was a hidden opening. If you got too close to it, and you weren't completely grossed out by the odor, you could find Smig.

"Psssst! Smig!" Leila called out. "Smig, it's me, Leila!"

A sewage-like aroma blasted forth, and Leila saw two beady eyes staring at her out of the darkness. "To what do I attribute the interruption of a perfectly satisfying postprandial nap?"

"Is my aunt Flora with you?" Leila asked.

"My dear, *what* are you insinuating?" Smig shot back.

"Never mind. I have to get to Knickerbocker headquarters. Can I get in this way?"

"I suppose so. But it's awfully small. And no one has used it in a while. You would have to walk through my private domain, you see. And I would request that you gave me adequate time to tidy up—"

"*I don't have that time, Smig. I'm worried Corey might be dead!*"

Now Smig's entire head emerged. "Oh dear! Well then, by all means—"

A scream cut off Smig in midsentence. "Leila!"

Leila spun around to see Bee sprinting down the path toward her. "Sorry! I hurried up as fast as I could! I saw you on the surveillance camera. Are you okay?"

"Where's Corey?" Leila blurted.

"I don't know!" Bee replied. "He's not with you?"

Leila sank to the ground. "He was sick. And bloody. I think someone shot him, Bee. I—I let him go out of my sight. He insisted. I never should have agreed. Then I got caught up with some escaped prisoners, and by the time I got back to him, Stanislaw and first-loop Corey had come through—and Corey, the wolf Corey, was nearly dead. Someone had shot him. He could barely speak. The only thing he could tell me was that he did nothing, Bee. But that doesn't matter. He can't be dead, okay? He can't be. We have to find him—now!"

Bee's thumbs were flying over her phone screen. "He never showed up at headquarters, Leila."

"He was with me! He had to show up somewhere!"

"Not necessarily," Bee said. "If something happened in the past to change history—"

"It didn't! When Corey said he did nothing, I'm

pretty sure he meant he didn't change history. And I didn't. I'm not a Throwback. And even if I were, I wasn't even in Kurtstadt. That was the only place where anything could have been changed! *We need to find him, Bee! You're a Tracker—tell me what happened!*"

"I'll be going now," Smig said, disappearing into his den.

"Okay, okay. . . ." Bee put her hand on Leila's shoulder. "I'm following everything you've told me. I understand—if Corey changed nothing, you and he should have returned to the exact place where you left. But maybe he wasn't as sick as you thought. Maybe he's nearby. Maybe he had to hide from the sight of tourists. In which case, he shouldn't be too far away. If there's a wolf in the North Woods Central Park, it won't be long before somebody finds him. I suggest we take a deep breath and go looking now—"

Leila's phone vibrated, and she jumped. "Sorry, I'm nervous."

"Take it," Bee said. "Maybe it's news."

Leila pulled out her phone and checked the notification on her screen.

Corey

Sup?

28

L eila felt faint. "This—this is a troll."

"What?" Bee said.

"Someone found his phone," Leila said.

"How do you know? Answer it, Leila!"

"He's a wolf, Bee, he can't text!"

Bee grabbed the phone and typed in a response.

> Where r u?

"Give that to me." Leila took the phone back and added to the conversation:

> if ur some troll jerk who just found this phone
> TELL THE TRUTH bc there is a life at stake no joke!!!

Leila held her breath until the response came back.

Corey

> Im at my house tapping out msg w
> my nose if u don't believe me its on
> w 95 st & you know the place so hurry
> im weak and need food maybe a squirel

Leila stifled a scream.

"What happened?" Bee said.

"It's him!" Leila replied. "He's still a wolf. But he's all right!"

"Wait. How can that be?"

"He's tapping the phone with his nose!"

"Leila, that doesn't make any sense—"

"*It's his address! It's his dumb sense of humor!*"

Leila shoved the phone into her pocket and raced out of the North Woods, with Bee close behind. She ran onto the transverse road and then wound her way down the park drive to the exit at Central Park West and 96th Street.

Corey's place was a brownstone on West 95th, just a couple of houses in from the park. She raced up the stoop and drew back her fist to pound on the door.

But it was already ajar.

Bee climbed the stoop behind her. The two of them were breathing like horses as Leila carefully pushed the door open.

The living room was dark. "Corey's mom and dad are probably at work," Leila murmured.

"Um . . . Corey's mom and dad haven't met," Bee said. "Because Corey's mom doesn't exist, remember?"

"What are you saying?"

"Maybe a prank?"

"How could it be a prank?" Leila snapped. "How would anyone pretend to be Corey if Corey wasn't born?"

"I don't know!"

"You're a Tracker! You *should* know!" Leila swallowed hard, peering warily into the room. "Corey? Are you—?"

"*AW-ROOOOOOOO!*"

The wolf cry made Leila jump back. She nearly knocked Bee down the stoop.

The room fell silent again and Leila leaned in. Her heart was pounding so fast she thought it might fly out of her chest. "Are you trying to be funny, Corey? What do you think you're proving? I swear, if you're playing some stupid game, I will never forgive you!"

When she got no answer, she barged into the living room and went straight to the floor lamp by the fireplace. As she flicked it on, the room was bathed in light. But she saw no one.

"Let's go," Bee said.

Leila inched her way back toward the door. From behind the couch came a low, angry growl.

Bee jumped. "Oh, good grief, my heart."

"Stop that!" Leila said. "Come out from—*aaaaaaah!*"

A giant figure leaped into the air and hurtled toward Leila. She felt Bee's hand grabbing her shoulder and pulling her away. Both girls tripped and landed on the carpet.

Leila flinched as a giant furry tyrannosaurus landed next to her.

"'The night Max wore his wolf suit . . .'" a voice intoned. And someone with a wolf mask rose up from behind the couch, clutching a phone.

Leila swallowed into a bone-dry throat and nearly barfed. She stood up and leaped onto the couch. Grabbing the mask with her right hand, she ripped it off.

With an explosion of laughter, a boy collapsed against the wall.

Leila felt the blood drain from her face. The boy

was all arms and legs, his hair rising from his head like an unruly bush. At first glance, he looked exactly like Corey.

At second glance, he still looked like Corey.

At third glance, Leila felt herself sucking back tears. "I don't believe this. . . . I don't believe this. . . ."

"I. Just. Can't," Bee said.

"What did you do, Leila?" It was Corey's voice. Not growly and mangled sounding.

It was Corey's smile, too. Human-Corey. Dressed in a dorky plaid shirt and jeans. As if nothing had ever happened. Before Leila could even think, she ran to him and wrapped him in the tightest hug she could manage.

He was alive. He was warm. His breath smelled of Mike and Ikes and his clothes of scented dryer sheets. She wanted to smack him for the prank. She wanted to tell him to brush his teeth and promise never to travel into the past again. She wanted to ask a gazillion questions.

But the smell was beautiful, she didn't want to let go of him, and honestly she really didn't care about the questions right now. The more he tried to shake loose, the tighter she held on, until he was about to push her away.

Then, without even thinking, she pressed her lips to his sweaty cheek and gave it a warm kiss.

"Ew, ew, ew," Corey said, pushing her away. *"Why did you do that?"*

Leila was grinning so hard her words sounded distorted, but she didn't care. "Because—because you're alive, Corey!"

Bee was cracking up. "Dude, I thought you were too old for cooties. She likes you. Get over it."

"Likes?" Corey said, wiping his cheek with the back of his sleeve. "Like, *likes*? Or *likes* likes?"

"I am not hearing this," Bee said.

"Corey, I—I *didn't do anything*," Leila said.

She stepped toward him, but he jumped back, banging against the wall. "You kissed me! That's disgusting."

"No, I mean in the past," Leila said. "In Germany. I didn't do anything that would have saved you."

Corey raced into the kitchen and returned with a damp paper towel. "Well, you must have." He wiped his cheek vigorously, staring at the floor.

"That's some thank-you," Bee drawled.

"I'm not a Throwback, Corey," Leila pressed on. "You changed nothing in the past and I wouldn't even have been able to change anything."

When he looked up, Leila noticed for the first time that his eyes were swollen and moist. "It had to be you. I told you, Leila, you are a Throwback."

"No, I'm not," Leila protested.

Corey's face was turning red. "Yes, you're not not!" he said, sticking out his tongue.

She could tell he was embarrassed about crying, which just made her want to embarrass him again. "Okay, stop it and be serious!"

"No! Because who cares how it happened!"

"Woo-HOO!" Now she was tumbling onto the sofa, pulling Corey after her.

This time he didn't push her away. He was screaming happily, too, doubling over with laughter. And as he fell to the floor, clutching his stomach, his tears were streaking both cheeks.

"Finally, signs of humanity," Bee said with a wry smile.

Impulsively Corey hugged Leila. When Bee raised her eyebrow expectantly and put her hands on her hips, he hugged her, too.

"Happy now?" Corey said, pulling back quickly. With a giggle, he wiped his eyes and gazed around the living room. "I—I just don't get it. I mean, this is the best thing that ever happened to me. When I woke up in Central Park, I thought I was dead. Like, in some Central Parky heaven as a human ghost."

"That makes no sense," Leila said.

"I know," Corey replied. "I ran straight here, because I could. My key worked, so this is my house. No one's here, but the same photos are on the mantel. And the bedrooms are all the way they're supposed to be."

"Which means you were born," Leila said.

"Duh," Corey replied.

"I mean, your dad married your mom," Leila continued, "which means your mom's parents were married, which means Helga must have gone to South America to meet your grandfather."

Corey shook his head. "But none of that should have happened. When I was a wolf, I saw Stanislaw and me. That was my chance! I could have done what we planned. But—but I didn't! I never talked to them. I never went with them to Kurtstadt. I shouldn't be here as a human. I shouldn't even be here as a wolf. I mean, *they shot me.*"

Leila felt her eyes welling up. She took a deep breath. "I thought I lost you."

"Bee, you're the Knickerbocker expert," Corey said.

"You tell us what happened."

"Well, we know your side of the story," Bee said, pocketing the phone and taking a deep breath. She sat across from them and held Corey's and Leila's hands. "I think it's best we take a minute to just enjoy. And then I want to know—exactly, minute by minute—what happened to Leila."

29

"Whoa, wait, Leila—you *met* Heinrich?" Corey said. "That Nazi creep who Stanislaw whacked in the head and left in the shack?"

He leaned forward in an armchair. Leila and Bee were on the sofa, facing him. The light was dim in the musty old room. Outside a car honked its horn, and the clock on the mantel ticked softly.

"Yes, in the woods," Leila said, "when you were off waiting for Stanislaw and first-loop Corey."

"Human-Corey," Corey said.

"Whatever. Heinrich was hiding in the bush. He showed me his head injury. I can't believe you didn't hear it. I could see you while this was happening."

"I was having a hard time keeping myself together."

"I know." Leila nodded. "Anyway, I drew Heinrich farther away from you. I was worried he'd try to kill you. He showed me the injury Stanislaw gave him. He wanted to find Stanislaw and kill him. He threatened me with a knife. I thought I was going to die right there, but I think he wanted to march me into Kurtstadt like some big hero. Maybe he thought he could murder us all together. He didn't know Kurtstadt was occupied by the Allies. So I played along. I figured when we got there—surprise!—the Allies would take him captive. Then I'd meet up with you and Stanislaw and Human-Corey and we'd get to work."

Corey nodded. "Not a bad plan."

"Yeah, but that blew up when we ran into a band of refugees from a concentration camp. Their leader was disguised as a Nazi. He lured Heinrich in, and then they all turned on him."

"Sweet!" Corey said.

"Not really. He nearly strangled this poor starving girl." Leila held up the Star of David necklace. "We managed to overwhelm him. She gave me this afterward. She said it would bring me luck. She was the one who grabbed a loose gun and shot Heinrich. For someone starving and nearly dead, she was really brave."

"She killed that creep?" Bee said. "Did you get her name?"

Leila shrugged. "I didn't ask. They were all exhausted. No one wanted to talk much. But I could hear the fighting in Kurtstadt already beginning. It turns out they were headed there. They knew it was an Allied stronghold. But they were all so vulnerable and weak, I couldn't let them go into a battle zone. So I told them to head to this other safe place they knew of, farther north. They left Heinrich there in the snow."

Corey's eyes went wide. "Wait a minute . . . that was him?"

"What was him?" Bee asked.

"Oh wow . . . way back when I first heard Stanislaw's story," Corey said, "Mom told me Stanislaw had found a gun . . . *near a dead soldier*, just before he got to Kurtstadt. That was the gun Stanislaw used to shoot at an approaching convoy that he thought were Nazis. They shot him dead."

"Which was the reason you went back in the first place, right?" Bee said. "To prevent him from shooting Allies by accident and save his life?"

Corey nodded. "Right. And I was with Stanislaw when we came upon the dead soldier, near a river. I distracted him. I didn't let him near the body. So he never took the gun. And I never turned the body over to identify it. I had no idea that guy was Heinie!"

"Okay, so I think I have all the information," Bee said. "But I still don't get it."

"What don't you get?" Corey asked.

"The answer to the riddle!" Bee went on. "You must have changed something, Corey. You're the Throwback."

Corey shook his head. "Nope. It was like a movie. When I was sitting at the bottom of the hill, feeling sick, *I realized I was the wolf I'd seen when I went back to save Stanislaw!* Right then I could have changed everything. I wanted to. But I couldn't bring myself to. I watched everything happen exactly the same way—Stanislaw and me, the same lines, the same things. It was a total, absolute repeat."

Bee shook her head. "It couldn't have been. I'm sorry, it just couldn't."

"Bee, I was the worst possible Throwback," Corey replied, "one who doesn't use his Throwback ability at all. There has to be another explanation."

A key slid into the front door and it opened. There, standing with a bag of groceries from the Mani Market, was an old man dressed in a long wool coat and wearing a Greek fisherman's cap.

Corey leaped up from the couch, grinning ecstatically. "Papou?"

The old guy laughed. "No, it's the Incredible Hulk. With an incredible backache. Will you take the groceries, *paithi mou?*"

"Woo-HOO!" Corey whooped, racing for his grandfather. "I am so so so so so happy to see you, Papou!"

Papou winked at Leila. "This is what happens when you buy race mice."

"*Ice cream!* 'Race mice' is ice cream, ha ha ha ha!" Corey blurted, grabbing the bags.

"This family is weird," Bee said.

As Corey headed for the kitchen with Papou, he asked, "Can I ask you something dumb?"

"There is no such thing as a dumb question!" Papou replied. "Unless it's a dumb question."

"So if I say the name Gregory, does it mean anything to you?"

"Is this a puzzle?"

"Sort of."

"Of course the name Gregory means something," Papou said with a shrug. "It means twenty-three dollars. That's how much that rotten Gregory Christopoulos owes me from the Super Bowl pool. But do you think

I'll ever see that? No! *Sto diavolo* . . ."

"Ha ha ha ha!" Corey shrieked. "Twenty-three dollars! Ha ha ha ha!"

"You must do something about that laugh, Corey," Papou said. "You sound like a hyena today."

As he went to hang up his coat in the closet, Leila smiled at Corey. Gregory didn't exist. In this loop, he never had. Corey's dad had married Corey's mom, Corey had been born, and Papou hadn't met his second wife.

"I hope old Fiona is happy, wherever she is," she said.

"I didn't like her," Corey murmured.

"Oh, by the way, *paithia*," Papou called out. "Will you put the ice cream in the freezer right away? You know how your *yiayia* hates melted ice cream."

Corey's eyes popped for about the fourth time. "So Yiayia's . . . *here*?"

Leila could tell he'd almost used the word *alive*. Saving his *yiayia* had been his first Throwback deed. But with all that had just happened, you never knew what was reversed and what wasn't.

"Of course, she's not here—don't be cheeky," Papou said.

Corey's face sank. "Oh. I'm sorry. . . ."

"Hi, Sorry, I'm Glad," Papou replied. "She works till seven o'clock on Thursdays, you know that! Now if you kids don't mind, I will briefly retire to the *mero* with the *Times* crossword puzzle while you put the groceries away. And if I'm not mistaken, your mother has just arrived with Queen Helga. She will need your help. *Ach*, one of these days we'll install an elevator!"

As he turned to go, Bee cocked her head. "*Mero?*"

"Bathroom," Corey said, shoving the ice cream into the freezer. "His favorite place in the house."

At the sound of the doorbell, they all left the groceries on the counter and raced to the front door. When they got there, Corey's mom was on the sidewalk. She was backing up a wheelchair to the bottom of the stoop. Her mom, Corey's grandmother, sat motionless in the chair. But she smiled when she saw Corey.

"Oh . . . Mutti . . ." Corey said. His eyes were filling with tears, and only Leila and Bee knew why. "Wow . . . I love you so much."

Corey's sister, Zenobia, looked up at him from the bottom of the stoop. She sneered in disgust, as if his face had turned green. "What happened to you? You grew emotions?"

Corey wiped his eyes. "I—I just—I don't know, she . . . looks especially beautiful, that's all."

"Corey, *bubbe*," Mutti said. "Give me a kiss. And a lift."

Corey jumped the whole stoop to land by her side, and he placed a kiss on her cheek. Then he, Leila, Mom, Zenobia, and Bee all lifted the chair up the stoop and through the front door. It was never an easy task. Mutti lived in an aging-care facility, and she was growing older and more forgetful by the week. Her eyes were filmy and she didn't smile much anymore. But Mom insisted that family time in this house made her happier than anything else.

In a few minutes, everyone was crowded onto the living room furniture. Papou put on the Greek music stream, Mutti howled that she wanted to hear "some nice polkas," and Zenobia disappeared into her bedroom.

It was the same every visit.

As the usual small talk began, Leila stole a glance at Corey. Their conversation about time travel had come to a screeching halt. She knew there had to be an answer. The result just seemed so . . . random.

So illogical.

He gave her a helpless shrug and she returned it. They could never broach the subject with Corey's mom. Or his dad or Yiayia or especially Mutti. Or Leila's mom.

Someday they could talk about this with Papou. He was a time traveler, too. And a puzzle expert.

But maybe the great riddle would never be solved. *Sometimes time will slip, Bee had told Leila. Think of how many things happen because of a slight mistake, a fraction of an inch, something unseen or barely heard. . . .*

Like the butterfly effect. An action so tiny it would be impossible to detect.

Leila took a deep breath and looked away from her best friend. Bee was deep in conversation with Papou about the crossword puzzle; Corey's mom was talking to his dad on her phone.

But Mutti was staring at her, looking lonely.

"Well, hi there!" Leila said. She gave her a big smile. You could never tell what Mutti was understanding or whether or not she recognized you.

"Dear Leila," she said. "Where did you get that?"

With a shaking hand, Mutti reached out toward her chest.

"My shirt?" Leila asked.

"The necklace."

Leila realized she was still wearing the necklace from her trek to Kurtstadt. "Someone very special gave it to me," she said, leaning toward the old woman. "A long time ago."

Mutti clasped the Star of David. For a moment her eyes seemed sharp and focused. "Yes," she said. "Beautiful. I once had one just like it."

Slowly she released the necklace and let it fall back. She looked into Leila's eyes, holding her glance for a long time, as if she were trying to remember something.

It was a bit embarrassing. Things often were that way around Mutti.

But Leila was noticing something on the old woman's face that she'd never noticed before.

A faded birthmark on her right cheek.

Now Mutti was losing focus again, sinking back into her wheelchair. Around her, everyone was gabbing. Papou was telling jokes Leila had heard a dozen times. Bee was laughing because she'd never heard them before.

But to Leila, it all seemed like voices from another dimension right then. She stared down at the Star of David she had now cupped in her own hand.

"Leila?" Corey said, scooching closer to her. "What's up?"

"The escaped prisoner," she said, her voice dry and parched. "The refugee. The one Heinrich nearly killed."

Corey nodded. "Right. The one who grabbed his gun?"

"She gave me this."

As Corey looked over her shoulder, Leila turned the Star of David around. On the back, two letters were engraved:

"Helga Meyer . . ." Corey murmured.

"It was her," Leila said. "One of those rescued prisoners on their way to Kurtstadt. A young girl."

"That was Mutti?"

Leila nodded. "In Kurtstadt, she would have discovered that her brother Stanislaw was alive. But she didn't. The prisoners didn't go there."

"You prevented them," Corey said. "You told them to go to the other place. Because of the fighting."

Leila nodded.

The plan to save Stanislaw had failed. But it didn't matter. No name had to be changed at any hospital. Stanislaw could be Stanislaw. Because his sister had headed to a different village. There, they would ship her to South America.

And Corey hadn't done a thing to make it happen. Leila had.

"I'm—" Leila said.

"Yeah." Corey nodded. "Yeah, Leila, you are."

"A Throwback . . ." Leila said the word softly, under her breath, testing how it felt. She liked it. She liked it very much. "You and me, bud."

"I was the first," Corey said. "Never forget that."

"But I," Leila said, "am the best."

The two of them burst out laughing so hard that everyone else's conversation ground to a halt. "Can you let us in on the merriment?" Papou said.

Before either of them could answer, the doorbell rang again. As Corey ran to get it, Leila followed.

He pulled it open to see an old man so hunched that he could barely look up. He was bone thin, but his shoulders were broad. As he strained to look at Corey, he flashed a grin full of obviously fake teeth. "Still climbing those steps all by myself!" he said proudly in a thick European accent that was vaguely German. "What do you say to that, eh?"

Leila watched Corey's jaw drop. "Uh, hi," he said.

"What is this 'uh, hi'? What kind of greeting is that for a man my age?" The old man gave Corey a bear hug and lifted him off the ground. "You see that? I love you, my boy. Oh, you know how much I love you."

Corey's face was bone white.

Now his mom was running in from the living room. "Oh, please, you're not supposed to travel alone!" she yelled. "What are you trying to prove? Where is your caregiver?"

The old man looked up from Corey. "Caregiver shmaregiver. You'll put me in a home yet. And they'll do to me what they did to my sister! Look at her. She was the strongest, loveliest girl in New York. Stronger than me. And now . . . pah!"

As the old guy shuffled into the house, Leila shot Corey a glance. *Who is that?* she mouthed.

Corey opened his mouth, as if to answer, but no sound came out.

Now his mom had the old guy by the arm. "Well,

Mutti will be happy to see you."

Papou stood from the couch and extended his hand. "Me? I'm happy you didn't kill yourself climbing the stoop, Stan."

Leila saw it now. She saw it in the eyes. She knew who this old man was. And one glance at Corey's face confirmed it.

"I've been through worse," said Great-Uncle Stanislaw.

The old man's voice, his accent, his broad shoulders, were unmistakable. Corey shot Leila a knowing look. *He sure has*, Corey mouthed.

He took Leila by the arm. Together they marched into the living room.

They stood at the threshold for a few moments. Leila looked into the face of Helga Velez, who had been Helga Meyer. In Leila's mind, it was easy to subtract the years. To see the incredibly brave young woman who escaped death and sailed across an ocean to start a new life. And Stanislaw, who had been near death as a young guy, had joy in every wrinkle of his face.

"Do you think he knows?" Leila whispered to Corey.

"Huh?" Corey replied.

"He met you in 1939," Leila said. "Exactly the way

you are now. Do you think he knows it was you back then who saved him?"

"Maybe he doesn't remember," Corey said. "It was a gazillion years ago for him."

When he looked back, Stanislaw was staring at them both. His face was all crinkled up in a smile.

Leila thought she could see him wink, but she wasn't sure.

No matter what kind of superpower you had, there were some things you would never know.

And maybe now, finally, you wouldn't want to go back and change a thing.

FOLLOW THE ADVENTURES OF

Jack McKinley in the mysterious, action-packed series that takes place throughout the Seven Wonders of the Ancient World.

For teaching guides, an interactive map, and videos,
visit **www.sevenwondersbooks.com**

READ THE FURTHER ADVENTURES IN THE SEVEN WONDERS JOURNALS

More adventures by PETER LERANGIS!

MAX TILT SERIES

THROWBACK SERIES

HARPER

An Imprint of HarperCollinsPublishers

www.harpercollinschildrens.com • www.shelfstuff.com